THE FIRE-HEART

Order Has a Cost

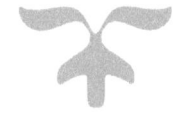

T. T. MANNING

Contents

Contents

N
E
W
S

Stonefield Village
Serenthall Village
City of Eldhar
Steelshore Village

Lanhua Village
City of Hanzhong
Zhiyé Village

Aegis Enclave
Guardian's Hollow
Arcane Peak
Faunacre Village
Elemental Grove

Chapter 1: Under Aurelian Rule

Thall had let his mother's soup cool. Not for lack of effort, but because each swallow asked more than he had to give. Since birth, five years past, illness had weighed on him.

He sat wrapped in a blanket near the hearth, knees drawn up, the bowl balanced carefully in his hands. Even when steam no longer rose from its surface, the scent still lingered. Root broth, thin and careful, stretched to last.

His pregnant mother, Althea, watched him from the table, one hand resting against the curve of her belly. She moved it away to tear the bread into pieces smaller than necessary. Thall swallowed slowly, each swallow took effort, but he did not complain.

The sound of wood against wood outside caught Thall's attention as it carried through the house in uneven bursts. His father's voice corrected without raising, steady and exact. Thall's older brother, Garrick, answered with quick movement, feet sure against the packed earth, a wooden blade snapping back into guard each time it was struck aside.

Thall listened on, envy threading through him as the rhythm carried a strength he lacked. His mother noticed and crossed the room, brushing her fingers once through his hair.

The sound outside changed.

Footsteps cut across the yard, heavier than the practice. Steel rang, not from training this time. Voices followed, low and formal. Thall heard his father speak once, not raised, not pleading. The words were spoken too softly to carry.

Althea rose too quickly and caught herself against the table, her voice sharp as she spoke his father's name while she pulled the back door open.

On the other side of the doorway, Dominion soldiers filled the frame, armor bright against the dim room. They had already crossed the yard.

One held his father by the arm, grip set hard enough to force his shoulder back. One of the soldiers turned to Althea. "Speaking against the Dominion has consequences."

His father's eyes caught Thall's. He was looking toward the hearth, toward him, before they pulled him back into the light.

◆ ◆ ◆

Thirteen years later, the village of Serenthall woke the way it always did, with care.

Smoke rose from cookfires that thinned and broke as the air warmed. Doors opened just wide enough for people to pass through. Voices stayed low, shaped less by fear than by long habit, by an understanding of who listened and what followed when someone did.

The village lay at the edge of the hills, where soil thinned and stone pressed through the ground in stubborn seams. Roofs clustered along narrow lanes worn smooth by feet and carts, their walls built from the same gray rock that surfaced in the fields. Beyond the last homes, the land rose sharply, scrub and shale giving way to the mountain paths that had once fed Serenthall's forges.

Before the Dominion, the village had been known for the fighting skills of its residents. Children grew alongside weapons, learning balance with a shield before letters, learning confidence from the weight of steel. Those lessons survived now only in recollection, carried in quiet stories and sentences left unfinished. Under the Dominion rule, that inheritance no longer marked pride. It marked attention.

The Aurelian Dominion had not come from beyond the horizon. It rose from this land, shaped by a single voice that gathered belief, hardened it into doctrine, and set it above blood and custom. Villages like Serenthall were folded into that order by its temples not as enemies, but as resources. Traditions were reclassified. People were sorted by obedience rather than place. What drew notice was corrected. What did not yield was no longer spoken of.

At the far edge of the village, past the first line of homes, wood met bone.

Garrick, now twenty one years old, struck Thall's shin with the flat of a practice wooden blade. "Again."

Garrick stood broad and grounded, feet set without excess motion. He did not rush. He did not retreat. His attention stayed on his younger brother, Thall, as he reset his stance, lighter in frame but no longer fragile, shoulders tight, weight carried too high.

Garrick stepped in and cut once, controlled and precise. The impact stung. "You're watching the blade," Garrick said. "Not the body."

Thall nodded. This time he widened his feet, bent his knees, and let his weight sink before he moved. Wood caught wood. The exchange stretched longer than before, each strike answered, each correction narrower than the last. It still ended the same way, Garrick's wooden blade resting where Thall's guard arrived too late.

Garrick stepped back and lowered his weapon. He stayed there, unmoving, close enough that Thall felt the pause settle between them. "You remember the winter you couldn't keep food down?" Garrick asked.

Thall blinked. "Barely."

"You were light enough I could lift you with one arm," Garrick said. "The doctor said you'd grow when you were ready."

Thall stayed where he was, blade lowered, waiting. "The others moved on early," Garrick said. "Heavier loads. Longer drills." He turned his blade once in his hand and set its tip against the ground. "You struggled when most of them didn't."

His gaze followed Thall's feet, the set of his hips, the way his weight stayed where it was placed. "You didn't rush it," Garrick said. "You worked with what you had."

Thall tightened his grip. "I had to."

Garrick's mouth shifted, just enough to show he had heard him. "You don't fall behind anymore."

"No," Thall said.

"Again," Garrick said, raising his blade.

◆ ◆ ◆

Inside one of the older homes, the shutters remained closed though the morning had climbed. The room had been cleared to the walls, its floor swept bare. Light pressed through the slats, striping the stone.

A circle traced the floor, thin and careful. The line broke where a hand had paused, corrected, then drawn again. It failed to meet itself.

Berrin, who was known to the Dominion as only a weaver, was secretly performing the rite of passage, meant to bless children and reveal their abilities. He bowed his head and placed his right hand over his heart, his left open toward the chalk circle. When he spoke, his voice carried across the room and drew the space inward.

"Solithar," he said, the words kept low, "who rises without summons and sets without leave, look upon what stands here."

The first child stepped forward. A girl with dark curls. Her mother's hand rested briefly at her back, then withdrew. The child crossed the chalk line alone and stopped at the center.

At Berrin's gesture, she turned and offered her back. "Show what was placed within her,". Warmth spread across the stone beneath the girl's feet. Light traced a path between her shoulders, slow at first, then narrowing as it took shape. The mark formed clean and precise.

"Dagger," Berrin said. "The child has an innate aptitude for daggers."

The second child approached. A taller boy. His father pressed a palm once between his shoulders, then stepped away. The boy entered the circle and turned as instructed.

"Let it take its own shape," Berrin said. The lines gathered broader this time, angling as they met. The symbol fixed itself with force enough to draw a breath from the room.

"Fist," Berrin said. "The child has an innate aptitude for hand-to-hand combat."

The third child waited at the edge. Her fingers clung to her father's sleeve until he knelt, freed them gently, and rose without looking back. She stepped into the circle, shoulders drawn tight as she turned.

"Let it stand," Berrin said, quieter now. The light hesitated. When it came, it cut fast and sure, the shape forming without correction.

"Sword," Berrin said. "The child has an innate aptitude for the sword."

Berrin lifted his head, breath drawn to speak again. A horn sounded outside, sharp and sudden. The children startled but did not move. The circle dimmed at once, its work complete. Berrin glanced towards the parents, already in motion. He crossed the circle toward the back, set his hands at each child's shoulders, and turned them one by one. Arms reached in, close and quick, parents did not linger. They took the children and slipped out through a narrow alley.

Berrin dragged his foot through the chalk, smearing the line until the circle lost its shape. The room emptied without pause, the sound of steps fading in uneven rhythm.

By the time the square filled, the knights were already there. They had come in without call and taken their places near the center, steel aligned, horses held just off the stone. Scripted lines cut into polished plate caught the light as they stood, each letter set with care. The Dominion's insignia appeared wherever it could be worked in, pressed into breastplates, stitched into barding, placed where the eye could not avoid it.

The mayor, Henry, crossed the square toward them. The villagers moved aside as he passed, no one needed prompting. He stopped before the lead knight and waited. The knight produced a parchment and set it into Henry's hands. Henry took it, turned, and faced the square. He cleared his throat once.

"Serenthall remains in arrears," he read. "Stonefield's ore shipments are delayed. Steelshore's forges remain incomplete. Yet resources continue to pass through this village without proper reconciliation."

He lowered the parchment and let his gaze travel across the crowd. "Order carries cost," he said. "What is taken must be answered for." A murmur rose, then fell away. Henry lifted the parchment again. "There are entries that should not exist," he read. "Rites conducted outside the rules." He folded the parchment once and set it aside. "That matter will be addressed." He turned and returned the document to the knight.

Not soon after, stalls opened in fits. A basket was placed back into place. Voices resumed in fragments, and the square began to move again, not together, but piece by piece. Henry turned and began the walk toward his house. The knights fell in behind him, steps striking stone in the same cadence until they cleared the square and were gone from sight.

◆ ◆ ◆

Darkness gathered over Serenthall in stages. Shutters closed. Lamps dimmed behind stone and wood. The lanes emptied until only a few distant steps carried, then ceased.

A knock came at Thall's window, light and deliberate. He opened it. His best friend, Eldrin, slipped inside at once. "They took Berrin."

Thall's jaw tightened. "When?"

"After," Eldrin said. "After people thought it was finished."

Althea turned from the table. "Keep your voice down. The walls have ears."

Eldrin nodded.

Eldrin had grown up in the orphanage. He was the same age as Thall, and they had stayed close since childhood.

"The orphanage doors will close soon," Althea said. "You should not be outside when they do."

"I know." Eldrin hesitated, glanced once at Thall, then backed toward the window. A moment later, he was gone.

Thall returned to the opening and remained there.

The street lay empty. No footsteps followed. No voices carried. The village did not stir again.

What quiet returned stayed drawn tight, as if waiting to be tested.

Chapter 2: The Weight of Silence

After the knights left, people spoke less.

Thall crossed the square mid-morning as the voices there thinned, hands tightened around tools. Some had turned away to occupy themselves with work that did not need doing. Stalls stayed open, fields were worked, repairs carried on, but each action came with care that had not been there before.

Near the market, Berrin's loom still stood where it always had, its frame catching the light. No cloth hung from it. Thall slowed without meaning to, then checked himself and walked on. Most passed without looking. One man paused long enough to say, low and firm, that rules existed for a reason. Another answered that faith required boundaries. No one dared to disagree. Corners stood empty where they should not have been.

One morning, Garrick stood at the board near the temple where escort work and field postings were nailed. He scanned the jobs, reached out once, then drew his hand back. After a moment, he stepped away and left the board unchanged.

Thall had taken the eastern path out of the village, following the line of fields until the road dipped and the trees closed in enough to hide it from sight. They had come here often, for different reasons, and none of them spoken aloud.

Eldrin crouched near a fallen log, a whetstone moving steadily along the edge of a small blade. He did not look up. "I passed the temple," Eldrin said.

Thall lifted his head. "So? What about it?"

"They hung a new banner." He turned the blade, tested the edge with his thumb, then set it back to the stone.

Thall breathed out through his nose. "They change them often."

"This one's larger," Eldrin said. "It hangs over the front arch. You can't see the stone anymore."

Thall turned and met his eyes.

"They don't want anyone thinking about what used to be there," Eldrin said.

Thall frowned. "Nothing was there." Eldrin held his gaze.

"That's the point." Eldrin rose, slid the blade into its sheath, and rubbed the white dust from his fingers against his palm. "I won't stay idle," he added.

"Eldrin, don't," Thall said. Eldrin had already turned back toward the village. Thall remained where he was a moment longer, then set off for the practice grounds.

Thall worked through the afternoon, feet setting, blade cutting, resetting again and again until his arms burned and his breathing evened. The forms stayed the same as he moved through them, weight and timing drawing his focus inward until little else remained.

◆ ◆ ◆

When the light thinned, Eldrin came for him and found him near the edge of the square. "Walk with me," Eldrin said, already moving.

Thall fell in beside him. "I don't like this."

Eldrin said nothing. They crossed the square without speaking.

Thall tried again. "You don't know who's watching." Eldrin kept his pace. His hand brushed once against the hilt at his side, then fell away as they moved on. "If it goes wrong," Thall said, "they won't stop with you."

Eldrin glanced at him once, gave a small nod, and looked ahead. They did not speak again until dusk stretched the shadows across the stone.

Near the well, Eldrin turned into the narrow lanes without comment. Thall hesitated, then followed, keeping distance, matching each turn as it came. The temple emerged as the light thinned to silver. Stone washed pale beneath the rising moon.

The new banner hung heavy against the front arch, its gold fabric catching what little light remained. The sunburst crest sat fixed at its center, precise and hard to ignore.

Eldrin stopped in the shadow and pulled his scarf up over his mouth and nose, leaving only his eyes.

"Don't," Thall said with a low voice.

"It's already decided," Eldrin replied.

Thall pressed himself closer to the wall, eyes tracking the street, then returning to Eldrin. Eldrin crouched and drew a small tin from his pocket, working the lid loose with his thumb. Inside, soot had been ground into a dark paste. He dipped his fingers and pressed them to the banner. His hand moved fast, the pressure even. Dark lines appeared against the gold, curving inward as they took shape. The Fire-heart symbol emerged under his touch.

A voice called from the far side of the arch. "Hey."

Eldrin broke into motion at once. As he crossed the edge of the light, a guard leaned forward, catching the movement. Boots struck stone and followed.

Thall stayed in shadow as the sound of pursuit pulled away down the lane. He waited, counting his breath, listening for a second set of steps that did not come. The banner still hung when he eased back into view. The mark remained. Rough at the edges. Impossible to miss.

The Fire-heart had been a title worn by the past rulers of the Eldhar Kingdom, given when authority was earned through oath and service rather than claimed by decree. It marked the one who had kept the lands together.

Under the Dominion, the title had been stripped from stones and struck from records. What it represented was left without place or voice, carried only where it could not be reached.

Thall did not follow Eldrin. He took the longer way home, staying close to walls and corners, listening for steps that never came.

Sleep broke apart more than once. When it finally took hold, it did not last.

◆ ◆ ◆

Morning found him moving toward the square before the choice had fully formed. The front of the temple stood open to the light. The banner that had hung over the arch was gone. Men were already at work.

The square slowed as people noticed the absence. Someone said the cloth had been taken down before dawn. Another said they had seen a soldier running after someone running near the arch in the dark. Words passed in fragments. One voice carried anger, sharp and open, calling it desecration. Another cut off short, eyes fixed on the arch before turning away.

The replacement was raised before the square filled completely. Thall was still hearing the murmur when Garrick's hand closed around his arm and pulled him back behind a house. Garrick drew in a breath through his teeth. "Were you there?"

Thall dropped his eyes and did not answer.

"Did anyone see you near it?" Garrick asked.

Thall shook his head.

Garrick held his gaze. "Wanting something doesn't protect you," he said. "When they come back, they don't stop."

"They already came," Thall said.

Garrick said nothing. His gaze shifted toward the road and stayed there.

◆ ◆ ◆

That night, Althea set Thall at the table and remained standing, her hands flat against the wood. "I taught you how to survive," she said. "Not to get yourself hurt, or worse, killed."

"I don't want Celestia growing up thinking this is normal," Thall said.

Althea closed her eyes. When she spoke again, her voice held, but her fingers pressed harder into the table. "That's what your father said, before..." The room went quiet around it.

"I'm sorry," Thall said.

Althea drew her hand back, then set it on his shoulder, firm rather than gentle. "I didn't say you were wrong," she said.

Thall stayed where he was after she left, the chair unmoved.

Next day, seeking his friend, Thall went to the orphanage first and asked. No message had been left. Outside the orphanage, near the bend where the trees thinned, something lay in the dirt where the ground had been disturbed. He knew the scarf before he reached it, the fabric worn thin along the edge.

He crouched, worked the mud loose with his fingers, folded it once, and slid it into the pouch at his side.

Whatever lay beyond that moment was his only hope.

Chapter 3: What the Dominion Notices

Thall returned home midmorning, dust still clinging to his boots. His sister, Celestia, was already there, pacing between the table and the window, stopping just long enough to look out before turning back again. She froze when she saw him. "Have you seen Eldrin?" she asked. "He hasn't been around."

Thall set his hands on the back of a chair but did not sit. "No."

She frowned. "That's not like him."

"He might have stayed out, I don't know" Thall said. His voice stayed level. "Gone somewhere off the road."

Celestia shook her head at once. "He wouldn't. Not without saying something."

Althea looked up from where she stood near the hearth. "Celestia."

"I'm just saying—" Celestia stopped, drew a breath, then tried again. "If he left, why wouldn't he tell us? If something happened—"

"Enough," Althea said, her tone calm and final.

Thall reached into the pouch at his side and drew out the scarf. He held it a moment longer than necessary before setting it on the table. Althea's eyes went to it at once. "Where did you find that?"

"Near the trees," he said. "By the bend."

She took it without comment, folded it once more, and set it aside. "That tells us very little," she said quietly. "Only that he passed through."

Celestia opened her mouth, then closed it again, after seeing the look on Thall's face.

Voices carried from outside. Boots followed, their rhythm even and aligned. Thall turned toward the window and did not look away. A Dominion patrol moved through the village at an even pace. They passed through the lanes and stopped where they chose. Stalls already cleared were checked again. Questions were asked without pause, and the soldiers remained where answers shortened and eyes lowered.

That's when Thall walked out, to watch from the edge of the street as shoulders turned and hands found work that could not be delayed.

Near the orphanage, the patrol slowed. The building came fully into view, its doors closed. One rider glanced toward it, then forward again, and the line resumed its pace.

At the far end of the lane, a herald appeared. He came and reined in beside the patrol on a black horse, its tack plain and kept to standard. The exchange was brief and carried no farther than the riders themselves. The patrol shifted at once, closing ranks around him. Together, they moved toward the square.

Mayor Henry was already there when they arrived, standing near the center where sightlines met. Space had been left open, and people were watching before the horse came to a stop. One of the patrol stepped forward and raised a horn. Its call cut clean across the square, and what movement remained fell away.

"The banner was desecrated," the herald said. "A mark was placed upon it during the night."

Henry inclined his head. "The matter is under review," he said. "Those responsible will be identified. Order will be maintained."

The herald's gaze passed over the crowd without pause. He unrolled a parchment. "Curfew is enforced from the second bell," he read. "Travel between villages now requires written approval. Implements intended for combat or training are to be registered and presented for inspection upon request." He turned the page. "These measures take effect immediately. Compliance will be noted. Failure will be addressed."

Thall stood among the others and listened. When the reading ended, the herald rolled the parchment and looked up. He held the pause, then turned away. People dispersed unevenly. Some nodded as they went, others delayed a step, eyes shifting, before breaking off and moving on.

Thall headed home. Garrick followed a short distance behind. Neither spoke on the walk back.

◆ ◆ ◆

They had just settled around the table when a knock struck the door. It came again at once. Garrick moved first. He opened the door and stepped partway into the frame, leaving no room to pass.

Henry stood on the threshold, two patrol soldiers set to either side. Their hands rested near their belts. "I need a word," Henry said. His gaze moved past Garrick and fixed on Thall.

Garrick paused, then stepped aside. The soldiers stayed where they were. Henry entered alone and took the seat at the table without asking. He set his hands flat on the wood and looked at Thall. "Thall." Henry then watched him for a moment before speaking. "Were you in the square last night?" His eyes studying Thall.

Thall drew a breath. "I was nearby."

26

"Did you see anyone approach the banner?" Henry asked. "Or anyone leaving the arch after?" Thall shook his head. "No." His voice low.

Henry did not look away. "You're certain of this." He studied Thall a moment too long. "Did you see anyone near the banner," Henry asked, "or anyone leaving the arch afterward?"

"I did not," Thall said. The word came slower this time.

"That's enough," Garrick said, stepping forward.

Henry raised one hand glancing at Garrick. "I wasn't speaking to you." His attention then returned to Thall. "Think carefully," Henry said. "What you recall later may matter more than what you recall now."

Thall swallowed. "I don't know anything."

Henry stood to leave, moving slow and deliberate. At the door, he paused and turned back. "If something comes to mind," he said, "it would be wise to report it."

When he stepped outside, the soldiers followed without delay, leaving behind them silence, and fear mixed with anger.

◆ ◆ ◆

That evening, Thall sat behind the house, where the village thinned into open ground. Eldrin's voice returned to him without shape or end, the last words cut short and starting again in his head.

When he could not stay there any longer, Thall went inside. Celestia had slept at the table, her head rested against her arms.

Althea rose as he entered. Walked over and kissed his forehead, rested her hand against his cheek for a brief moment, then bent and lifted Celestia. She did not speak again. Thall went down the hall as Althea carried Celestia toward the back room.

The other room, one he shared with Garrick was dim, the lamp burning low. Garrick lay back against the wall, awake. He turned his head as Thall entered. Thall walked then sat on the edge of his bed. For a moment, neither of them spoke.

"I should have stopped him," Thall said.

Garrick let his breath out. "You tried."

Thall looked at his hands. "If I had been firmer—"

Garrick shook his head once. "Then it would have been someone else." He paused. "The Dominion doesn't wait." The lamp guttered between them. "When you see the edge again," Garrick said, "you'll know it."

Thall nodded.

Garrick reached over and turned the lamp down.

Darkness filled the room. Neither of them spoke.

Chapter 4: The Cost of Promise

Morning spread through Zhìyé before the sun cleared the hills.

The fields filled early now. People arrived while the air still held its night cool, tools already in hand, moving with the quiet efficiency of those who knew the work would only grow heavier as the day went on. Shortening daylight pressed against every task, though no one said so aloud.

Zhìyé lay in the southern reaches of the Lianhua Dynasty, where authority moved through custom rather than decree, carried intact from one generation to the next. Nothing here needed to be announced to be enforced. People knew where to stand, when to bend, when to yield space without being told.

Terraced rows of herbs stretched outward from the village, orderly and deliberate. Each bed was bordered by low stone walls worn smooth by decades of hands bracing there, knees pressing there, baskets set down and lifted again. Nothing grew by accident. Nothing was tended without reason.

Sakura moved through the rows with a basket hooked at her side, its weight pulling steadily against her hip as she worked. At fifteen, her hands knew the labor well enough that she did not have to think about it. She checked stems before cutting, brushed soil from roots before lifting them free, and left untouched what was not ready.

Care guided her movements. Waste troubled her more than fatigue ever had.

Ahead, her mother Anya worked more slowly than she once had. She stopped often, resting one hand against her knee or steadying herself on the stone borders between rows. The cool morning air helped, but not enough. Sakura noticed each pause and said nothing.

Behind them, her older sister Mira crossed the terraces toward the storage shed, two sacks balanced against her shoulder. Her pace stayed steady. When the weight pulled unevenly, her jaw tightened and she shifted the load higher without stopping.

"Leave that one," Mira called without turning. "It needs more time."

Sakura checked the plant, then altered her path.

Mira rolled her shoulder once and continued on, already counting what could be finished before the bells. "I need to wash," she said. "If I'm late again, they'll mark it."

She didn't wait for a response.

Mira reached the wash basin first. Water splashed as she scrubbed dirt from her hands and wrists. She dried them on her skirt, stepped inside long enough to change, then returned with her hair bound and sleeves fastened. She was halfway down the lane before anyone else had finished their rows.

The village bells rang, marking the start of the school day.

By then, Sakura's basket stood half full, her shoulders aching beneath the familiar strain. She welcomed the ache. It meant she had done something that mattered.

◆ ◆ ◆

By midday, movement extended beyond the fields. Merchants crossed the outer paths with carts drawn low beneath their weight. Zhìyé was known throughout the Dynasty for the quality of its herbs and staple crops. Caravans rarely left lighter than they arrived, and lately they asked for more than before.

The school sat along the eastern road, modest and practical, meant for children who would return to fields and workshops when lessons ended. The temple stood closer to the village center, its pale stone walls marked with symbols meant to instruct rather than intimidate.

Sakura paused at the edge of the fields and watched students pass along both paths. Some turned toward the school. Others toward the temple gates. A few walked in pairs, murmuring as they went.

Some looked her way, then turned elsewhere.

Anya noticed. "You're watching again."

"I wasn't," Sakura said, though the denial came too quickly.

Anya did not press her. "It doesn't change anything," she said instead.

Sakura nodded and returned to her work.

When the sun climbed higher, Anya lowered herself onto the stone border and stayed there. Her breath shortened, uneven. She lifted a hand when Sakura moved toward her.

"You need to rest," Sakura said.

Anya smiled faintly. "Later."

Sakura knelt beside her anyway and rested her fingers against her mother's wrist, intending only to steady her. Warmth gathered beneath her touch before Sakura recognized it, spreading without pattern or command.

Anya's breathing eased, just enough to find its rhythm again.

"You shouldn't rely on that yet," Anya said, her tone gentle but firm.

Sakura pulled her hand back at once. "I didn't mean to."

"I know," Anya said. "That's why you have to be careful."

She covered Sakura's hand with her own, her palm warm and steady.

"We never had the means for temple study," Anya continued quietly. "The lessons demand time away from home, and the cost follows long after."

Sakura looked down at her hands.

"The training teaches control," Anya said. "Without it, even careful use can go wrong. And once people notice ability, they expect more than a child can give."

The space between them carried that truth without further comment.

The warmth was familiar to Sakura. It had first been named during her Coming-of-Age Rite, when she was five and the village gathered in quiet observance before Mother Nature, Shurén, to witness what blessing had emerged. Light had traced the space between her shoulders and resolved into the butterfly mark, a sign of healing affinity recognized throughout the Dynasty.

Since then, it surfaced quietly. A cut that closed before it should have. Pain that eased sooner than expected. Plants in her rows that held longer, rooted deeper, without being pressed.

None of it drew comment in Zhìyé. Blessings often took the form of ability, distinct in shape and strength, and were treated as part of growing. Families guided them with care, keeping instruction close to home, speaking of them only when delay itself became a risk.

The temple representative arrived that evening without announcement, finding them at the edge of the fields. He had come before. Sakura's name had been recorded more than once. The temple kept careful account of its practitioners, and that account had grown thinner than it preferred.

He spoke calmly and without urgency. "We have fewer trained healers than we once did," he said. "When ability appears beyond the temple's direct care, response becomes our responsibility."

His gaze rested on Sakura only briefly. "She shows strong aptitude," he said. "The kind that requires guidance."

Anya listened without interrupting.

"The temple can provide that guidance," the man continued. "The education is demanding."

"And costly," Anya said.

The man inclined his head. "And time sensitive."

Silence lingered before Anya said, "Give us time."

The representative did not press the matter. He left without setting terms.

◆ ◆ ◆

As the light faded, the day's labor ended. Tools were gathered, baskets cleared, and the fields left behind. Sakura walked home with Anya, the house closing around them in a quiet that pressed inward.

Mira returned later, her satchel hanging loose at her side, dust clinging to her hem. She stopped when she entered, taking in the room at a glance.

"He came," she said.

Anya nodded once.

Mira set her satchel down and drew a breath. Her eyes moved to Sakura, then back to their mother. "So," she said. "It's time."

"We are past that," Anya replied.

Mira leaned against the table, grounding herself. "I've been late to school more often than not," she said. "The lessons run long, and they cut into the fields."

Her fingers then traced the satchel strap. "It helps," she said more quietly. "But things wouldn't fail without it." She hesitated, then lifted her gaze. "If the temple is asking whether Sakura's ready—"

She stopped, swallowed, then continued. "I can step away from the village school."

Sakura turned toward her. "No."

Mira shook her head. "I can work full time. We'll manage."

"That isn't fair," Sakura said, her voice tightening. "I didn't ask for this."

"No," Mira said. "It's still here." She paused. "Ignoring it won't spare any of us."

Sakura shook her head. "I don't want it if it costs you this."

Mira's smile formed slowly, thinner than before. "Then it would be wasted," she said. "And the cost would be greater."

Sakura had no answer.

Sleep came late and lightly. She lay awake as the village hushed around her, distant bells fading, herbs rustling as they dried, her family's breathing close and steady.

Her thoughts returned to the temple and to leaving, to being seen for reasons she did not control. None of it found a place to rest.

By morning, one truth remained. Going would not allow hesitation. It would not be hers alone.

She returned to the fields as the sun rose, moving carefully between the rows. The land felt steady beneath her hands. Familiar. Honest.

Beyond the terraces, the road toward the temple lay open.

Life continued, not unchanged.

Chapter 5: The Measure of Worth

Sakura rose before sunrise, when the road would still be quiet and fewer people would notice her leaving.

The decision had settled during the night, not as certainty but as absence. There were no more paths left to consider. She dressed without lighting a lamp, moving by memory through the small room she shared with her sister.

Anya was already awake.

She packed the satchel with the same attention she gave to market goods, folding each garment neatly, smoothing creases that would not matter once the road dust settled. She set aside what would not be needed, weighing each item once before placing it in Sakura's hands.

Mira checked the straps and adjusted the weight so it would rest evenly across Sakura's shoulder. She tugged once, then again, testing the balance.

"It will hold," Mira said. "It carried my books for years. Just don't overload it."

"I won't," Sakura said, though she wasn't sure what counted as too much.

They walked together to the stone marker where packed earth gave way to road. Zhìyé was already stirring behind them, smoke lifting from hearths, tools striking stone in steady rhythm. The village sounded the same as it always had. That was what made leaving feel sharper.

Anya stopped first. She rested her hand briefly against Sakura's arm, her grip firm rather than lingering.

"Listen more than you speak," she said. "Ask if something is unclear, and remember what you're told."

Sakura nodded.

Mira lingered a moment longer. "Be careful with yourself," she said.

"I will."

Mira's mouth curved into a small smile. "I won't be late anymore."

Sakura stepped forward before either of them could say more. This time, no one followed.

The road narrowed as it climbed, winding past terraces she had worked when she was small. Stone markers appeared more frequently as the fields thinned, each carved with the seal of the Lianhua Dynasty. Hanzhong guards stood where the road widened, offering direction without urgency. Travelers moved freely, though rarely alone for long.

◆ ◆ ◆

By the time the sun cleared the hills, Zhìyé lay behind her.

Hanzhong rose ahead.

The city stood larger than anything Sakura had known, its stone pale and clean, its paths laid with intention. The central temple dominated the skyline, rising alongside the castle, its presence felt long before its details came into focus.

Inside the temple grounds, movement carried a different weight. Students crossed the courtyards with purpose, voices low and steps unhurried. No one ran. No one lingered without reason.

Sakura was directed to a narrow office set off the main hall. A clerk sat behind a low desk layered with ledgers, their spines worn smooth by handling. Other students waited along the wall, younger than she was, shifting their weight as they watched the door.

The clerk studied Sakura's papers longer than she expected.

"You're older than most who arrive here," he said at last.

"I haven't had temple instruction," Sakura replied.

He nodded once and wrote something down. "Then you'll begin below your aptitude until the record supports advancement."

"How long?" she asked.

He closed the ledger. "Your progress will decide."

An attendant led her from there to a small room shared with three other girls. The beds were identical, each chest locked, names carved above the doorway. Hers had been added recently, the carving shallow and precise.

"You'll meet with an assessor in the morning," the attendant said. "Until then, settle in."

Sakura set her things away carefully. The others glanced as she entered. One nodded. Another leaned back to make space near the wall.

"You're in the last bed," one said, already returning to her work.

"Thank you," Sakura replied.

The room returned to routine as lamps were lit and books set aside.

She lay awake as the light faded; the steady breathing of her roommates close by. The weight of leaving pressed against her chest, familiar and unresolved.

◆ ◆ ◆

Morning came quickly.

The days that followed took shape quickly. Morning lectures, evening review, work that advanced in small, repeatable gains. Adjustments appeared in her schedule without explanation. Her name moved between columns in ledgers she rarely saw.

One evening, a quiet whimper came from the next bed over, uneven and cut short.

"It doesn't stop," a girl whispered. "The lessons move too quickly."

Sakura waited before answering. When the sounds eased, she asked, "Which part are you stuck on?"

"M—mana manipulation," the girl said.

Sakura crossed the room and retrieved a folded note from her desk. She placed it in the girl's hands without comment.

"You can borrow it," she said. "Return it when you're done."

The girl nodded. "Miko," she said. "From Lánhuā."

"Sakura," she replied. "From Zhìyé."

By the end of the year, Sakura followed the same instruction as those seated beside her. Her work met expectations. Her name appeared where it was meant to.

In her second year, incantations were introduced. Training advanced from recognition to use, from sensing to shaping, always under supervision. Sakura was placed where steady hands were needed, her assignments given and recorded without comment.

"You're from Zhìyé?" an instructor asked once, watching her work.

"Yes."

"That explains the discipline," he said. "Mind your pace. Others are still learning."

"I understand," Sakura replied.

Work that required correction drew attention. Work that did not was given more of the same.

The practicum took place in a smaller hall; its stations arranged in a shallow arc so the instructor could observe without moving far. Each table held identical materials, measured and prepared in advance. The task was simple: stabilize a simulated wound, maintain the seal, then withdraw without overcorrection.

Sakura worked at the second table from the end. Miko stood beside her, shoulders tight, hands hovering too close to the focus point.

"Slow," Sakura said quietly.

Miko nodded, though her fingers did not ease. The incantation faltered midway, warmth rising unevenly before slipping.

"Again," the instructor said from the center of the room.

Miko drew a breath and restarted. This time the warmth surged too fast, pushing past the boundary the exercise required. The seal thinned.

Sakura moved before she checked herself.

Her hand did not touch Miko's. It hovered beside the focus, steadying the flow where it wavered. She adjusted the cadence, quiet and precise, guiding the warmth until it held. Then she withdrew at once.

The seal stabilized.

The instructor crossed the room and stopped at their table.

"Acceptable result," he said. "The sequence was broken."

He turned to Miko. "You hesitated, then rushed."

Miko swallowed. "Yes, sir."

"You will repeat the exercise after the session," he said. "Twice."

Then he looked at Sakura. "You intervened."

"Yes," Sakura said.

"Did you request permission?"

"No."

He inclined his head. "You stabilized the outcome. That is not in question."

He paused. "This exercise exists to teach process. When you intervene, others stop learning."

"I understand," Sakura said.

"You will be assigned to preparation work during future practicums," he said. "This maintains consistency."

She inclined her head and stepped back.

From the edge of the room, Sakura watched the practicum continue. Miko worked through the repetitions more slowly now, posture corrected as needed. The instructor spoke only when required.

The seal held on the third attempt.

When the session ended, the group was dismissed in order. Sakura remained long enough to return tools and clear the table.

Miko found her near the doorway.

"I didn't ask you to," she said.

"I know."

Miko hesitated. "It helped."

Then she left.

That evening, a notation was added to Sakura's record without comment. She read it once and returned the ledger.

Later, in the shared room, Miko lay awake, staring at the ceiling.

"They told me I'm improving," she said quietly.

"You are," Sakura replied.

A pause followed. "They didn't say anything about you."

Sakura set her things in order. "They didn't need to."

◆ ◆ ◆

By her third year, the pattern no longer surprised her.

During private practice, she pressed her palms together and recited the incantation softly, feeling warmth rise in response to attention rather than impulse. She guided it until it steadied, then stopped.

Alongside this, she began formal study in medicinal alchemy. Ingredients were prepared with the same care she once gave the fields at home, remedies brewed in stages, effects observed and recorded rather than forced.

"How do you keep it so even?" Miko asked once.

Sakura considered the question. "I don't start until it feels right," she said. "If I reach too early, it pushes back."

When permitted, she tended the small herb plots along the outer paths. Over time, the plants she worked grew fuller and steadier than the others. No one commented. Sakura noticed and left it there.

When her work was finished, she lay back in the shade and closed her eyes, listening to her breath slow and the ground hold firm beneath her.

The temple asked only for consistency.

Learning how to provide it without drawing notice became part of the discipline.

Chapter 6: Quiet Distinctions

By the middle of her third year, Sakura no longer checked her schedule to know where she was expected.

Her days settled into patterns that did not announce themselves until they were already established. Most of her hours were spent in the herb rooms, spaces set apart from the instruction halls and observation chambers. The work there favored timing over speed, attention over force. Growth was supported within narrow limits, corrections made early and without emphasis.

Where Sakura worked consistently, the plants filled out more fully. Stems held under their own weight. Yields arrived earlier and with fewer losses. No notation followed the difference. The records reflected output, not cause.

Requests reached her without announcement. Tasks accumulated where her hands proved reliable. Tools and materials appeared closer to her station. When something moved, she was told once and expected to adjust.

Healing no longer required rehearsal. Incantations were spoken deliberately and only when needed, shaped with enough force to act and stopped before they could extend beyond their purpose. Recovery followed clean lines. Adjustments grew fewer.

What changed was not difficulty, but expectation.

When other students faltered, instruction slowed. When Sakura did not, the pace increased. She was given work that demanded restraint rather than repetition, tasks that left no margin for display.

Her attendance in certain lectures became irregular. She remained assessed and corrected when required but was more often directed elsewhere. During sessions, she assisted rather than participated. Preparatory work filled the gaps, keeping her moving between rooms while others stayed seated. The assignments were not framed as consequence or distinction. They were recorded as a need.

During her third year, she was assigned to assist in the kitchens.

The work began during a shortage and continued after her name remained on the roster. Instructions were given once. Corrections were brief. When tasks were completed, she was dismissed.

No one asked about her standing. They asked whether she could lift the crates from storage, whether she could return when deliveries ran late, whether she could stay when the count came up short.

"You've done this before," one of the older bakers said, watching her set a basket down without spilling its contents.

"At home," Sakura replied.

The baker nodded and turned back to her work.

Sakura stayed until the heat bled from the room and the last trays were cleared. On those nights, she slept more fully and left only when released, not when the work appeared finished.

Her instruction hours compressed around the kitchen schedule. When she asked whether the changes affected her standing, Professor Shūmei answered without looking up from his ledger.

"Your record reflects completion," he said. "Location is irrelevant."

She returned to her work.

Shūmei noted it again during a later review, his eyes passing briefly over the flour on her sleeve.

"You've been assigned outside the halls," he said.

"As needed," Sakura replied.

He closed her file and dismissed her.

◆ ◆ ◆

As her third year ended, interruptions became routine. Rooms changed without notice. Materials she prepared were taken up by others before she returned. When she arrived early, she was sometimes asked to wait until space became available, even when the room stood open. She treated the delays as part of the task.

Questions received answers. Silence followed when none were asked.

Her results remained consistent.

Midway through her fourth year, Sakura was summoned to a small office near the central hall.

The Lead Temple Priest, High-Priest Liang, reviewed her ledger in silence before closing it.

"You are ahead of schedule," he said.

Sakura waited.

"There is cause to conclude your instruction here earlier than anticipated," he continued.

"What would that require?" she asked.

"Less time learning here," Liang said. "More responsibility elsewhere."

She inclined her head.

"Advancement reduces your time as a student of this temple," he said. "It does not reduce your burden."

He paused only long enough to let the words settle.

"Your tuition has been settled in full."

Sakura remained still.

"You are cleared for reassignment beyond study," he said. "You will not remain in the halls."

"What will I be assigned to?" she asked.

"Supervised healing service," Liang replied. "Consistency and restraint will take precedence over continued training."

She inclined her head.

"You are authorized one week's leave," Liang added. "Afterward, you will report back for placement. Compensation will be issued and recorded alongside your service hours. A portion will be retained for oversight."

"When does the leave begin?" Sakura asked.

"Immediately," he said.

She inclined her head once more.

She crossed the halls at an even pace and returned to the quarters she shared. Inside, she closed the door and stood still before moving. Her belongings were packed quickly and with care. What she did not need, she left arranged as it had been. What remained fit easily into the satchel she had carried here years earlier.

She did not wait for the bells.

At the outer road, a merchant wagon stood ready to depart, its crates sealed and stacked with care. The driver waited beside it, checking lashings by lantern light.

"Are you headed south?" Sakura asked.

The man straightened. "As far as Zhìyé," he said. "Corvin Holt. Holt Trading."

"Sakura," she replied. "If you have room."

"I do," he said, already making space. "It's a quiet run."

She climbed up as the wagon rolled forward.

"You're headed home," Corvin said once they were moving.

"Yes," Sakura replied. "I haven't been back in some time."

The road passed in long, quiet stretches, broken by the creak of the wagon and the steady turn of wheels. When Corvin asked about her work, she said only that her training had been completed. When he asked where she would be placed next, she told him she would learn that after her return.

What she spoke of more freely was Zhìyé. The fields at first light. The house kept in motion by her sister's steady presence. Her mother's hands never truly at rest, even when she was.

Corvin listened without interruption.

They reached the crossroads after the moon had claimed the sky. Sakura asked to be let down, lantern light pooling briefly against the packed earth before the wagon moved on.

She followed the familiar path to the house and knocked once before opening the door.

Warmth met her at once. Mira turned first, disbelief crossing her face before she crossed the room and caught Sakura in her arms. Anya followed, her hands firm at Sakura's shoulders, drawing her in without words.

For a moment, no one spoke.

Then the house filled again with movement—voices overlapping, steps crossing, the sound of a place that had kept space for her all along.

Chapter 7: Open Ground

Faunacre did not build walls.

Homes stood apart by pasture and field, their paths worn by feet and hooves rather than stone. Fences appeared where animals required them. Beyond that, the land remained open, kept by habit and use.

The village lay within the Kingdom of Aetherwind, where people were known more by what they tended than by what they commanded. Tamers worked alongside their animals in farming, hunting, and husbandry. Summoners called on elementals only what daily labor required. Trust carried farther than structure, and when it failed, the failure showed quickly.

Thorne crossed the eastern pasture at a steady jog, bow slung over one shoulder, boots dark with mud from the low fields. A brace of small game hung from his belt.

Near the tree line, he slowed and whistled once.

His hound, Ashe, emerged from the brush a moment later, low and broad through the shoulders, her coat mottled to match the undergrowth. Her ears stayed forward, eyes alert, tail still.

"Good," Thorne said, resting a hand briefly against her flank.

She leaned into his touch, then turned her attention back to the field.

They headed toward the fence line together.

Beyond the enclosure, his father Rowan, leader of Faunacre, stood near the posts as two mud elementals worked the soil in steady silence.

The mud elementals are little more than moving masses of mud, their shapes swelling and slumping as they advanced. Where they pressed forward, the earth yielded, folding and releasing as deep furrows formed behind them.Beyond the enclosure, his dad, the leader of Faunacre, Rowan stood near the posts as two mud elementals worked the soil in steady silence. Their forms moved low and deliberate, earth folding and releasing beneath them as furrows deepened.

He stood watching his wife, Taya, as she moved along the fence, her rounded belly narrowing the space as she guided a pair of yearlings toward the far pasture. She paused at the gate to correct the latch, then continued without looking back.

Rowan glanced toward her, then returned his attention to the elementals.

"You took the long route," he said.

"Wind turned," Thorne replied.

Rowan nodded once. "You adjusted."

He dismissed the elementals and joined Thorne as they crossed toward the yard.

At the yard, where the temple's posting board stood beneath the awning, Thorne unhooked the game and set it on the scale. The clerk marked the ledger and tied a tag through the cord without looking up, then counted out payment and slid it across the table.

Rowan waited a few steps back. When Thorne turned away with Ashe beside him, he followed without comment.

They passed the storage sheds at the pasture's edge, nodding to two younger tamers hauling feed and a woman coaxing a stubborn mule forward. Rowan acknowledged them in passing and kept walking.

Inside the open shed, Rowan moved along the wall, checking harnesses and feed stores by habit. Bows hung from pegs, some worn smooth with use, others newly strung. A few spears rested near the door, their shafts marked by training rather than battle. Thorne moved a step behind him, adjusting arrow bundles and checking leather straps as Rowan passed.

"Corvin Holt passed through late," Rowan said. "Didn't stay."

Thorne paused with a strap in his hands. "Corvin?"

"The trader," Rowan said. "Comes through a few times a year."

"I know the name."

Rowan adjusted a spear back into its rack. "There's more talk on the road."

"About the Dominion?"

"It's closer," Rowan said. Then, after a moment, "Closer doesn't always mean louder."

Thorne nodded and finished with the strap.

◆ ◆ ◆

The horn sounded just before midday, sharp and urgent, from the southern ridge.

Thorne moved at once. He took his bow, signaled Ashe, and cut across the slope toward the sound. Two older tamers and a pair of young summoners followed, but he reached the ridge first.

A cart lay overturned near the ravine. One horse was tangled in the traces, panicked and bleeding. The other had bolted. The driver stood frozen, hands loose at his sides.

60

Thorne approached slowly, voice low. "Easy."

The horse's breathing came hard and uneven.

He cut the straps cleanly and freed the animal, pressing his palm to its neck and staying there until the tremor eased and the movement slowed.

Rowan arrived moments later and took in the scene. His gaze moved from the driver to the ravine, then back to the horse.

"You did right," he said.

He knelt, one hand at the shoulder, the other behind the jaw. Arcane energy gathered between him and the animal. Beneath his touch, the locked muscle eased. The bleeding slowed but did not stop entirely.

Rowan withdrew his hands.

"We don't mend," he said. "We patch them, the healer will do the rest."

He nodded toward the runners. "Get word to the yards. Have a healer come this way. The cart won't move yet."

Thorne stayed with the horse while the message went out, keeping his hand where the animal could feel it. When the shaking returned, it passed more quickly this time.

◆ ◆ ◆

By evening, the pasture quieted. Thorne sat near the fence with his bow across his knees, cloth moving along the limb in slow strokes. Ashe lay beside him, head down, watching the field.

Rowan joined him and lowered himself to the ground with a soft sound. He set a wrapped bundle at Thorne's side.

Thorne untied the cloth. Dried meat and a heel of bread, still warm. He tore a strip free and passed it back. Ashe took it gently and returned to her place.

"From Taya," Rowan said.

Rowan's gaze rested on the bow.

The memory returned without invitation: a ring of packed earth at the temple, elders spaced evenly, names spoken once. When Thorne stepped forward, there had been no pause. The mark had formed cleanly, shaped like a bow.

"Father Time, Vekran, gave you a clear sign," Rowan said.

Thorne continued working the cloth along the limb.

"You'll be called on more," Rowan added. "Not because things are wrong. Because they keep moving."

Thorne nodded.

After a while, Rowan spoke again. "Before these fences were mine to mind, I walked beyond them. Guardian's Hollow was one of the places I passed through."

"The village to the north," Thorne said.

Rowan's mouth tightened slightly. "They act faster there."

"They push harder." Thorne argued.

"They leave less room," Rowan said. "That's not always worse."

Thorne considered that, then said, "I know what I'm responsible for."

Rowan watched the animals cross the field, unhurried. "Then you'll know when restraint stops being enough."

They sat without speaking as the sky darkened and the first lamps appeared across the village.

When Thorne rose, he crossed the yard to the archery field. The targets stood where they always had, their faces worn by years of use rather than neglect.

He set his feet and loosed arrow after arrow. The first two struck true but wide, thudding into the outer rings. He adjusted his stance without thinking and loosed again. The third landed centered.

He kept shooting until the motion steadied his breathing and quieted his thoughts, the bow bending clean beneath his hand, the rhythm returning to something familiar.

Ashe lay a short distance off, watching the field rather than him, ears turning with each sound that did not belong.

When he paused and lowered the bow, the yard held its stillness. The fields beyond lay quiet. No one called out. Nothing moved that should not have.

Thorne stood there a while longer, bow at rest, and understood what the open ground asked of those who kept it.

The road beyond Faunacre lay open, unchanged in the fading light.

Thorne looked back once, not at the fields, but at how close the road had begun to feel.

Chapter 8: Beyond the Familiar

The road out of Faunacre was narrow, more suggestion than structure.

Thorne followed it at first light, packed light, bow secured, Ashe moving a few steps ahead. He matched her pace without thought, shortening his stride where the ground dipped, lengthening it where the path opened. Balance came from attention, not force.

Behind him, the village thinned without marker or gate. The land simply changed.

Rowan's words stayed with him, as did Corvin's warning. What had once sounded distant now carried weight through proximity rather than rumor. Faunacre taught its tamers to respond when balance failed, not to wait for danger to announce itself.

The fields gave way to scrub and broken stone as the road climbed. The air sharpened with rise and distance. Faunacre did not fence itself in, but neither did it extend welcome beyond its ground.

Ashe slowed first.

Her tail lowered. Her ears turned outward, tracking ahead. Birds fell quiet, and the wind brushed the grass without carrying sound.

Thorne stopped before the road narrowed.

He dropped into a crouch and studied the ground ahead, not the road itself but the way it narrowed between stone and brush. The slope favored anyone waiting above it.

Thorne stayed still and listened.

Voices carried from ahead, low and impatient.

Thorne made a brief motion with his fingers. Ashe slipped into the brush without sound.

One voice muttered, "He said this was the busiest route."

Another replied, "Then he lied."

Thorne edged forward, keeping downwind as the ravine opened below. The road narrowed there, stone and root closing it tight. Three figures stood near the crossing, armored but mismatched, their insignia scratched away. One held a hound at his side, its posture loose but watchful. Their attention drifted.

A fourth figure knelt near the overturned cart, bound and bloodied, struggling to stay upright.

Thorne took the ground in with a glance. The slope favored anyone waiting above it. Brush closed one side.

The road left no room to spread out. Ashe waited at his flank.

He waited for the right moment before he loosed.

The arrow struck the nearest man in the shoulder, knocking him back with a shout.

The group broke apart. One spun toward the sound. Another tore a blade free. The wounded man lurched away from the cart as the hound surged forward, startled into motion.

The man with the blade lunged.

Ashe broke for the third man instead, hitting him low and hard and driving him off balance as the blade came through where Thorne had been standing.

Thorne loosed at the hound as he stepped sideways, taking it down, the blade grazing his ribs as he tried to dodge.

Pain flared along his side. He stayed upright, adjusted his stance, and loosed again. The arrow passed cleanly over Ashe's shoulder and struck the fallen man before he could recover.

Ashe turned back toward the man with the blade, then checked herself as the last man broke and ran.

She drove into him before he could clear the brush, slamming him hard into roots and briar and tangling his limbs as he went down. Thorne loosed a final arrow, finishing what Ashe did not.

Silence returned, uneven and short-lived.

Thorne stood long enough to bring his breathing back under control, then moved. The road remained narrow, and sound carried.

He kicked the blade from the fallen man's reach and bound his hands. He secured the one struck by the first arrow as well, ignoring the curses forced through clenched teeth as the cord tightened. When they were tied together near the tree, he pressed cloth to his side until the bleeding slowed, the sharp pain limiting his movement but not stopping it.

Only then did he turn back.

Ashe returned to him, eyes clear, body unmarked.

"Good," Thorne said quietly, resting his forehead against hers for a moment.

The bound figure near the cart stirred. Thorne cut the ropes and eased the man upright. He was older, shaking, his breath uneven.

"Corvin Holt," the man said hoarsely. "Holt Trading Company."

"Thorne." He inclined his head.

Corvin's eyes moved over him, taking in the bow, the hound, the torn bramble at his shoulder, the way he favored one side. He said nothing about it.

"Bramble clan," Corvin said after a moment. "Rowan's kid."

Thorne nodded.

"You passed through Faunacre," he said.

"Stopped east," Corvin replied. "Had business to finish."

Thorne glanced down the road. "Guardian's Hollow?"

Corvin nodded. "That was the plan."

Thorne waited while Corvin settled himself, then secured the two injured men to the back of the cart. He adjusted the knots once, then again, when his side pulled at the movement.

"Ready to ride?" he asked.

"Slowly."

"Then we move."

Thorne helped Corvin onto the cart and took the reins himself. He kept his eyes on the tree line, not the road.

The horse stepped forward at once, pace even.

◆ ◆ ◆

Ashe moved ahead of the cart, keeping to the road's edge.

They did not go far.

The road dipped into low ground and narrowed as brush closed in. Ashe slowed, posture tightening.

Thorne caught it a breath later. The brush ahead went still.

He guided the cart closer to the ravine wall, leaving less room on one side but more sightline ahead. The adjustment cost him time, not distance.

A snarl cut the quiet.

Wolves burst from cover, ribs showing beneath matted coats, moving together.

Thorne stepped between Corvin and the wolves and drew. Sharp pain pulled along his side as he raised the bow, forcing him to lower the angle and shorten the draw.

Ashe met the charge head-on, driving one wolf back before turning on another.

Thorne loosed twice in quick succession. One wolf fell. Another veered away, wounded and yelping.

The rest pressed in, the cart limiting retreat.

Ashe took a glancing hit to the shoulder but kept her ground, placing herself between the cart and the wolves.

Ashe lifted her head. Her chest filled, and the howl broke from her, long and carrying, cutting through brush and stone alike.

The pack hesitated, momentum breaking as they went still.

Movement answered from the ridge behind them. A large hound stepped into view, broad through the chest, a pale scar crossing one eye. He paused, assessing the space rather than the threat.

His pack surged from cover, disciplined and fast. He drove into the attackers at their head and broke the charge with speed rather than noise.

When the wolves scattered, the hound met Ashe's gaze once, recognition clear, then turned and led his pack back into the trees.

Ashe remained where she was, blood darkening her fur along the shoulder. She did not pursue.

She returned to Thorne's side and sat.

"You could have warned me," Thorne said quietly.

Ashe flicked an ear and licked at her wound.

Corvin let out a breath. "That wasn't chance."

"No," Thorne said. "It wasn't."

They moved on once the horse calmed. Thorne kept the reins steady, favoring one side now without comment.

By dusk, they reached a ridge. Smoke rose ahead, thicker than hearth fires, stone walls and watchtowers catching the last light.

"Guardian's Hollow," Corvin said.

Ashe growled low.

Thorne kept his eyes on the walls ahead.

The road did not widen to meet them, and he did not expect it to.

Chapter 9: Hollow Ground

Guardian's Hollow did not open itself to strangers.

The road dropped into a narrow ravine before reaching the walls, stone pressing close on either side. The settlement rose from that cut in layered tiers, built into the slope rather than spread across it. Watchtowers stood along the upper ring, their silhouettes clear against the fading light.

The gates stood open just wide enough for passage, set between stone jaws that guided traffic inward and left little space to wander.

Thorne guided the cart forward at a steady pace. Corvin sat beside him, quieter now, eyes tracking the walls. Beneath the tarp in the back, the two bound men rustled against the boards, their breathing uneven, blood darkening the cloth beneath them.

"So this is it," Corvin said.

Ashe moved ahead of the cart, pace even. Her ears turned as figures repositioned along the walls. She did not look up.

A horn sounded from the battlements, low and controlled.

Spacing tightened along the wall. Attention turned inward. The gate narrowed by a fraction.

Two guards stepped onto the road. One moved with a sabretooth at his side, the other directing a void elemental. Neither looked at the cart at first. Their attention stayed on the space around it.

Thorne drew the reins and slowed, easing the cart into the lane they indicated.

"Corvin Holt," one guard said. "You're injured."

"The road wasn't clear," Corvin replied.

Corvin gestured toward Thorne. "He saved my hide, twice. Three men waiting at a crossing. One didn't walk away."

The guard's gaze went to the tarp. He noted the bindings beneath it, the spacing between the bodies, then returned his attention to Corvin.

"Then there were wolves," Corvin added. "A pack."

The guard looked to Thorne, taking in the bow, the hound, the way he stood with the reins loose but ready. He gave an approving nod.

Two handlers detached from the inner yard and took position just inside the gate.

"Bring the cart through," the guard said. "Slow."

The sabretooth beasts moved first, opening a path.

◆ ◆ ◆

Inside the walls, the space opened into ordered yards and training rings. Beasts moved under signal rather than voice. Elemental forms responded to controlled gestures, their movement precise and contained. Corrections came quickly. No one raised their tone.

Corvin watched it all as they passed. "They take over fast," he said.

"That's the point," Thorne replied.

They had gone only a short distance when a broad-shouldered man with iron-gray hair crossed their path. His stride was even. His attention moved across the yard, then returned to the cart.

"Secure the prisoners," he said.

Two tamers broke from a nearby ring at once.

"Food and rest for the merchant," he added. "Have him seen to, then help him secure the cart."

Corvin inclined his head. "Thank you, Master Roland."

Handlers took the cart. Corvin stepped down and before he followed them, he turned to Thorne.

He reached into his coat and drew out a small leather purse, weighing it in his hand. "For the road," he said, offering it toward Thorne.

Thorne shook his head.

Corvin studied him, then extended the purse again. "You took wounds keeping us upright."

"I took them doing what needed doing," Thorne replied.

Corvin held the purse a moment longer, then nodded and drew it back.

"You kept us moving," he said. Not thanks. Just fact.

Then he went with the handlers.

Only then did Roland turn to Thorne.

Roland's eyes moved over him, taking in the bow, the hound, the way he held himself despite the wound at his side. His gaze lingered on the Bramble crest caught at Thorne's shoulder, still clinging there.

He looked to Ashe, to the confidence she commanded, to the way she remained alert without anchoring to Thorne.

Roland nodded once.

"Bramble clan," he said. Not a question.

Thorne inclined his head.

"Faunacre," he said.

"Yes."

Roland's attention returned to Ashe. "No wonder she's well handled," he said. "Control like that is taught early."

He studied Thorne a moment longer. "Are you planning to stay?"

Thorne did not answer at once. "I don't know," he said finally. "I wanted to see what lay beyond Faunacre."

Roland considered that.

"If you choose to remain," he said, "we can use you."

He turned slightly, already shifting back into command. "You'll rest. If you choose to stay, you'll be assessed at first light. Until then, you don't train, and your hound stays with you."

Thorne inclined his head. "Understood."

"Peace lasts," Rowan said, "until someone decides it's worth breaking." Roland turned away, already issuing instructions as he went.

◆ ◆ ◆

Later, near the outer wall, Thorne cleaned his bow. Ashe lay beside him, alert but resting. A shallow cut along her shoulder had been cleaned and bound with leaf and resin, the scent sharp and familiar.

Nearby, a young female tamer worked the same way, then eased her fox into a resting crouch.

"Healing is limited," she said. "We keep what can still work."

Thorne nodded.

"I overheard you earlier," she went on. "You can remain here. Train. Learn how we operate."

Thorne continued running the cloth along the bow.

"And if I leave?" he asked.

She looked toward the ravine. "Then you leave knowing how narrow the road becomes."

"I'll know by morning," Thorne said.

She nodded once. "May I?" she asked, gesturing toward Ashe.

Thorne glanced down. Ashe watched her without tension.

He inclined his head.

She knelt and scratched behind Ashe's ear. Ashe leaned into it, steady and unguarded.

"She looks content," she said. "Even when hurt. Not on edge like the others."

"Faunacre," Thorne replied.

She considered that, then rose. "Does that make a difference?"

"Do you think it does?"

She smiled faintly. "I was taught there are many ways to maintain a blade. Some temper with heat. Others keep the edge with oil."

She glanced once toward the darkened yard. "It's late."

Then she turned and walked back along the inner paths.

Thorne finished cleaning the bow and set it beside him. Ashe remained at his side, eyes open, breathing even.

Beyond the wall, the ravine darkened.

Inside it, the yard stayed in motion.

Chapter 10: The Sea-Salt Cage

Lea was already awake.

She lay still on the narrow cot, listening as sound moved through Aegis Enclave, carried along stone corridors and across open courtyards, rising and falling with the wind that cut along the cliffside rings. Footsteps passed overhead. Metal rang once, then again, then faded.

She did not rise until the row monitor passed.

Aegis Enclave was not built for comfort. Thick walls kept the chill of the sea pressed close, salt clinging to the air as platforms jutted from the cliff face, each marked with Aetherwind sigils worn thin. Below them, waves struck stone without rhythm or pause.

It was a settlement pressed into the cliffs, shaped by need rather than intention. Summoners and tamers lived side by side, their paths diverging only where function required it. Instruction took place where space allowed. Experiments were conducted where containment could be maintained. Those without families worked because work was expected.

Aetherwind's orphanage stood within the Enclave, guiding those without families toward work and assigned purpose. It was arranged around intake, instruction, and placement, its routines set long before Lea arrived.

Lea rose, folded her blanket square to the cot's edge, and joined the line moving through the passageways.

She took her place at the outer ring, where those assigned to structured invocation were arranged. Some stood taller, others filled their robes more fully. She wore the same training cloth, and the same admission marks etched into the bracelet at her wrist.

The instructor took count and moved directly into instruction.

"Focus," the instructor called. "Control depends on restraint."

Lea closed her eyes and aligned her stance with the seam beneath her feet. Her breathing slowed until each inhale matched the last. A small ember formed between her palms, no larger than a coin, its edge clean.

Around her, other constructs swelled unevenly. Heat rolled across the ring. One student reached too far. Steam hissed as a construct collapsed and dispersed.

The ember wavered as her breath shortened, then steadied between her palms.

"Compliant," the instructor said, already moving on.

The exercise ended without comment. Names were called once. Pairs were dismissed and routed toward secondary instruction or assigned labor.

◆ ◆ ◆

Lea followed her partner toward the mess hall.

The meal was thin broth and coarse bread. The girls sat shoulder to shoulder along the stone tables, eating in intervals marked by the scrape of bowls and low voices kept beneath the room's echo.

Linara, seated beside her with her own bowl untouched, slid half her bread toward Lea without turning. "I'm not very hungry."

Lea tried to push it back.

"They added you to the outer list," Linara said. "You'll need it."

Lea paused, then accepted it with a single nod. "Thank you."

Linara acknowledged it with a brief nod.

Lea inclined her head.

When the bowls were cleared, names were called again. Lea's came near the end. She was directed to the outer ward.

The ward housed bound elementals within active seals. Fire and air, water and stone rested within their lattices, their forms moving only within assigned limits. Ward runes glowed faintly along the stone.

Lea worked without speaking. She recorded fluctuations, reinforced stability where the resonance thinned, and adjusted the seals when the glow along the runes dimmed unevenly.

It was during one of these checks that she noticed the bird.

It perched along the rail beyond the ward, dark-feathered, wings drawn close. Birds gathered near the cliffs. This one did not move when she approached. Its head angled slightly. Its attention remained.

Lea paused. "Go," she murmured.

The bird chirped once and stayed.

She returned to her work. When she looked again, the rail was empty.

Midday brought drills.

Students rotated through paired summoning exercises. Each was tasked with forming a bound construct and maintaining cohesion under strain. Lea's partner lost control early, the fire thinning as its outline wavered.

Lea adjusted her footing and slowed her breath. The flame drew inward, tightening into a birdlike shape that remained intact.

The instructor watched from the perimeter. "Again."

They repeated the exercise. Lea corrected her balance. The construct endured longer this time.

When they were dismissed, the instructor motioned her forward.

"You adapt instead of asserting," he said. "Invocation requires structure."

Lea lowered her gaze. "Yes, sir."

He looked at her a moment longer, then turned away.

◆ ◆ ◆

Evening brought stillness to the Enclave. Lamps burned low along the corridors. Wind struck the shutters in uneven bursts. Somewhere below, a contained resonance carried faintly through the stone.

Lea sat on her cot with her hands resting on her knees.

Summoners summoned. Tamers tamed. The division should not be crossed.

The girls returned from drills and baths, splitting off in groups and pairs. Lea stepped onto the narrow balcony beyond the dormitory and rested her hands against the stone rail. Below, the sea stretched dark and uninterrupted, pale foam tracing the cliff's edge as wind moved freely at that height.

A bird settled on the rail a short distance away.

It was dark-feathered, its wings drawn close, similar in size and coloring to the one she had seen near the ward earlier. Lea did not speak. She remained where she was.

The bird angled its head, watching her. It showed no sign of alarm.

Footsteps sounded in the corridor behind her, a brief movement of voices passing the open doorway. Lea turned at the sound.

When she looked back to the rail, the stone was empty.

She remained there until her breathing slowed.

When she turned back inside, the corridor had thinned. Voices carried downward toward the bathhouse carved into the lower stone. Steam rose through narrow vents, carrying the scent of mineral water and soap worn thin by use.

Inside, voices softened as robes were set aside and the girls eased into the pools.

Lea lowered herself into the water beside Linara. Heat spread through her shoulders. The stone edge caught faintly against the calluses at her palms.

Linara leaned closer, brushing ash from Lea's forearm. "You missed some."

"Thank you."

"It's sticking lately," Linara said.

Lea nodded. "The outer rings run hotter."

"They always do." Linara hesitated. "You were there again."

Lea nodded once.

"How long?"

"Long enough." Lea said with an exhale.

Linara quietly protested. "That's not right."

"I entered the library outside assigned hours," Lea said.

Around them, small gestures passed between the girls. Laughter surfaced briefly, then faded. Linara remained angled toward the water.

Lea rose from the pool and dried herself while Linara's eyes stayed on her.

That night, the Enclave quieted in layers. Contained resonance threaded faintly through the stone.

Lea lay still as the lamps dimmed. Her hand moved to the drawer of the stand beside the cot. She drew it open and took out the small pendant, the only keepsake her mother had left her.

Her fingers closed around it as she held it tight.

When she returned the pendant to the drawer, her movements were slow.

She remained awake a moment longer before sleep took her.

Chapter 11: The Bond and the Bound

Lea was crossing the upper corridors along the outer route as assigned when the sound reached her, water striking stone with force enough to carry through the walls.

She continued toward the ward, pace unchanged, the damp edge of heat trailing along the floor beneath her feet.

Beyond the threshold, the elemental containment ring glowed unevenly, runes along the stone thinning and brightening as strain pulled them out of alignment.

Inside the ring, a water construct surged against its boundaries, its mass folding inward before breaking outward in violent waves that struck the field and rebounded.

The other rings remained intact.

Lea hesitated at the threshold.

The construct surged again. Water slammed against the containment field, rattling the rails. The glow thinned, then caught by a narrow margin.

She looked once down the length of the ward, then back to the ring, and stepped forward.

Her shoulders lowered as she aligned her stance with the stone beneath her feet. She raised her hands, palms open. Her breathing slowed, each draw shorter than the last, as her arcane reached outward and made contact.

The resistance was immediate. Pressure built as the construct pushed and recoiled, its mass moving without pattern. Lea kept the invocation narrow, adjusting as the force surged and withdrew, the control thinning, then returning, never fully settling.

Boots struck stone behind her.

"Hold," an instructor called.

Lea did not release. She maintained the boundary for a brief span before the pressure climbed again, the water pressing hard against the containment.

Professor Grey stepped in beside her. His arcane aligned with hers at once. The pressure shifted. Under his influence, the construct drew inward, its movement tightening along defined lines.

Lea lowered her hands and stepped back, breath catching once before she steadied it.

Another instructor arrived and turned sharply, blocking the ward entrance. "Clear the perimeter," he ordered.

Grey remained until the construct quieted. The nearby instructor moved in at once, replacing the compromised runes along the ring.

He stepped back at last. His gaze paused on Lea, unreadable, then moved on.

The incident was recorded later as rune degradation. Wear over time was cited. Maintenance intervals were adjusted.

◆ ◆ ◆

During secondary instruction, the hall quieted as students took their seats. Summoners and tamers sat together, the distinction marked only in the ledger, not in placement.

Lea sat with her hands folded on the desk. Linara took the seat beside her.

"I enjoy being a tamer," Linara murmured, barely moving her lips.

Lea inclined her head.

"I choose summoning," Lea replied just as quietly.

Linara exhaled, as if setting the thought aside. Neither of them looked away from the lectern.

Evening brought the mess bell. The hall filled before Lea arrived, long tables crowded with bowls set close together. The meal was thinner than midday, porridge barely warm, roots mixed through for weight rather than taste.

Lea set her bowl down. Linara glanced at it, then slid half her bread across the table.

Lea hesitated and pushed it back.

"After what happened earlier," Linara said. "You'll need it."

Lea broke the bread and ate.

Across from them, a younger girl leaned forward, spoon forgotten. "I saw birds again," she said. "Down by the lower wall."

"They never stay," Linara replied.

"I know," the girl said. "I still like watching them."

Linara nodded once. "I wish I could get close to one."

Lea kept her eyes on the table.

The bell rang again. Bowls were cleared. Names were called, Lea was assigned to stable oversight.

The scent reached her first, hay and fur undercut with iron. Animals shifted as she passed, some pressing back, others watching. She kept her pace even, her presence narrow.

High along a support beam, a familiar bird perched in stillness, dark-feathered and alert. It did not move when she looked up.

At the far end of the row, a horse lifted its head. Its ears angled forward. It released a low breath, curious rather than alarmed.

Lea slowed. "That's enough," she murmured, the words coming from habit rather than decision.

The horse lowered its head again, but its eyes remained on her a moment longer before turning away.

Her hand lifted, then fell back to her side.

She finished her checks quickly and washed at the basin near the exit, scrubbing until the smell dulled.

The library lamps were lit when she arrived. Linara was already seated, reading, her materials spread in an orderly stack before her. Lea took the opposite place and set out her own volumes.

"Thank you for bringing mine," Lea said quietly. Linara nodded without looking up.

They worked without speaking, pages turned carefully, notes copied line by line.

Lea finished first. She returned her materials and reached for a volume from the nearby shelf. The title was stamped plainly along the spine.

Tamer's Bond and Summoner's Bind.

She read until the evening bell sounded. Linara closed her folio at the same moment. They left together.

That night, Lea lay awake longer than usual. The keepsake turned slowly between her fingers, warm from her touch. The memory of the ward returned, pressure building where it should have eased. The horse's attention followed, lingering where it should not have.

The words surfaced as they always did, learned early and repeated often.

Summoners summoned. Tamers tamed. The division should not be crossed.

Sleep came eventually, the sounds of the Enclave carrying faintly through the stone.

Chapter 12: Forgotten Legacy

The lecture hall was half full. Students sat in rows without grouping, tablets open, eyes forward.

The instructor spoke from the front without raising his voice.

"Summoners and tamers are not limited to field application," he said. "Placement varies by aptitude and endurance."

He marked the slate behind him with short lines of chalk.

"Summoners are most often assigned to structural reinforcement, containment maintenance, and controlled invocation. Tamers find placement in transport oversight, beast handling, and perimeter response."

He paused, then added another mark.

"Keepers fall outside both categories."

Several heads lifted.

"Keepers are arcane users blessed by Vekran, Father Time, assigned to recovery and stabilization," he continued. "They do not heal in the conventional sense."

The chalk tapped once against the slate.

"Herbal compounds are used to support the body's own processes. Arcane application assists by reinforcing tissue integrity and regulating strain. It does not restore what has been lost."

He turned slightly, addressing the room.

"This differs from the healers blessed by Shurén, Mother Nature, whose methods rely on incantation and resonance. Their practice is not taught here."

No one spoke.

"Keepers are trained to preserve function," he said. "Not to reverse damage."

He erased part of the board and continued on.

The summons came without notice.

Lea was pulled from evening study and directed toward a smaller instruction chamber set apart from the main halls.

She entered a room with one table and two chairs. Shelves lined the walls, their reference volumes too brittle for common use.

Instructor Grey waited inside.

He was older than most, his robes faded by years rather than neglect. Iron-gray ran through his hair. He moved with careful economy; each step placed before the next.

"Take a seat," he said.

Lea complied, quietly and quickly.

"You've been consistent," Grey said. "Adaptable."

She quietly nodded.

"That tendency," he continued, "draws attention when it alters outcomes."

"My record should show compliance," she said.

"It does." Grey reached behind him and took down one of the older texts. The spine cracked faintly as he opened it.

"You've been reviewing material beyond your assignment."

Lea did not answer.

Grey turned the book toward her. Two circles were drawn in faded ink, overlapping only at their edges. Sigils marked each, one set rigid, the other responsive.

"Both disciplines operate under the same permission," he said. "What differs is application."

Lea leaned forward slightly, then stopped.

"When instruction overlaps too early," Grey continued, "students lose precision. Focus degrades. Endurance fails."

"So separation prevents loss," Lea said.

Grey did not answer at once. He closed the book and rested his hand against its cover.

"Separation simplifies oversight," he said.

She waited.

"The body can extend its arcane capacity toward binding or toward bonding," Grey added. "It cannot sustain both."

"Those who attempted it reached neither," he said. "The record is consistent."

"I did not—"

Grey rose. "That is all for tonight."

Lea inclined her head. "Thank you."

Grey offered no reply.

She left the chamber and did not return to the dormitory. Her steps carried her downward instead, toward the lower library.

The room was unheated, lit by narrow windows and oil lamps that cast uneven light along the shelves. This was where the older records were kept. Volumes had been repaired more than once. Margins carried signs of revision.

Lea pulled books in sequence, scanning entries.

Successions   recorded   without   detail.
Affinities   noted,   then   left   unexplained.
Wild   elemental   constructs.
Shapes of the arcane.

One volume sat apart from the rest, its pages thin and brittle. Lea turned them carefully until a single entry broke the pattern.

It concerned a prince from an early reign, bound to a drake in accordance with rite. The bond was recorded as stable.

Further on, the same hand recorded the prince's pursuit of structured invocation alongside the bond. The language narrowed there, avoiding speculation.

The result was instability.

The decree that followed prohibited divided regulation within a single practitioner. The wording emphasized prevention, not judgment.

The record moved on, but the prince did not.

Lea leaned back from the table.

She returned to her dormitory long after the lamps had dimmed.

◆ ◆ ◆

In her room, sitting at the edge of her bed, she reached beneath her pillow, her fingers closed around the keepsake she had carried since childhood, smoothed by years of handling. Whatever markings it once held had been worn down until they could no longer be read at a glance.

She turned it once, then again, slower this time.

The shapes from the worn etchings returned without invitation. Circles. Edges that did not fully align. Her thumb traced grooves she had never examined closely before.

She stopped.

The engraving was faint, nearly worn away, and did not match the arcane circles she had been taught. Its lines lacked the rigidity of invocation and the responsiveness of bonding, resting between the two.

Her breath left her in a single, shallow pull, and the room felt smaller.

She closed her fingers around the stone. It felt heavier than it had moments before, familiar and difficult.

The arcane pressure stirred from her, slipped outward in a narrow bleed, brief and uncontrolled, shallow and unformed. The stone answered it.

Her mother's presence surfaced without image, a hand at her shoulder and a voice, low and resonant, within her head.

Pressure gathered low in her chest. Without pain or strain.

Warmth spread along the pendant's surface. A dim edge of light surfaced, uneven and short-lived. Lea drew back at once, but the response had already passed through it.

For a moment, the room thinned.

Something moved at the edge of her awareness. Neither a construct, Nor a beast. Its outline resisted coherence, proportions failing where they should have aligned.

Lea remained still.

Summoners summoned. Tamers tamed. The division should not be crossed.

The words surfaced fully formed, unchanged, and insufficient.

She lay back against the cot, the stone clenched in her palm.

Whatever the records claimed, this place did not carry all of it.

And whatever had been missing, it had not begun with her.

Her thoughts were interrupted by a knock at the door, light and uncertain.

Lea rose her head. Before she could answer, a voice followed, low.

"It's Linara."

Lea crossed the room and opened the door. Linara stepped inside, closing it behind her.

Lea's hand then moved to her collar. She drew the pendant up and tucked it beneath her shirt.

Linara noticed her face. "You look worried," she said.

"I'm just tired," Lea replied.

She sat at the edge of the cot. Linara remained standing a moment longer.

"May I join you at the cot," she asked.

Lea nodded.

Linara sat beside her. The space between them narrowed but did not close.

"Happy birthday," Linara said.

Lea blinked. "That's today."

Linara gave a small nod. "I don't have a gift. I just wanted to make sure I came by."

"Thank you," Lea said.

Linara leaned in, her eyes closed and her cheeks flushed.

Lea drew back.

The moment hung, unfinished. Linara stopped, then straightened at once. "I'm sorry," she said.

She moved for the door, opening it quickly. Lea lifted her hand as if to speak, but nothing followed. Linara was already gone.

Lea closed the door and returned to the cot. She lay back and stared at the ceiling.

The sound of waves carried in from below, steady against the stone. After a time, the rhythm pulled her under.

Chapter 13: Tended Lands

The road into Hanzhong curved gently downward heading south, trading stone for packed earth and cultivated paths. Thall noticed the change immediately. The land felt tended rather than guarded. Fields were marked by low boundary stones instead of fences, irrigation channels kept in careful order, water flowing steadily through stone-cut grooves without spill or waste.

The distance did not trouble him. In Serenthall, strength came from repetition and necessity, shaped by work that demanded endurance rather than display. Travel followed the same rhythm.

He adjusted the strap of his pack, brushed his fingers with the stiff edge of the sealed letter tucked inside, and continued on.

The Dominion's reach did not end here; it only grew thinner. There were fewer banners, soldiers stood farther apart, but faith in the Dominion remained steadier than its presence ever had.

The road narrowed as Thall approached the boundary marker. Two stone pillars stood opposite one another, weathered but unmistakable. A small Hanzhong temple detachment waited nearby, not in formation, but positioned with intention. They wore the crest of the Lianhua Dynasty at the shoulder, simple and worn from use.

"State your purpose," one of the soldiers said, stepping forward. His tone was bored rather than hostile.

Thall presented his sealed message without comment.

The soldier did not open it. He checked the seal, compared the mark against a ledger, then returned it with a curt nod.

"Welcome to Hanzhong," he said.

Thall inclined his head once and passed between the pillars. With each step, his shoulders eased. His stride lengthened. The Dominion did not vanish behind him, but it no longer pressed at his back.

He had been sent with purpose, though with no explanation, a message carried from Serenthall's temple to the outer temple districts of Hanzhong. Routine on the surface. His hands lingered on the seal longer than necessary.

The road widened as it carried him into Hanzhong proper, low buildings gathering along the street in pale stone and clean lines. Ast beneath shallow awnings, voices carrying easily as people moved with purpose but without watchfulness, paths crossing and separating in a way that required no careful calculation.

◆ ◆ ◆

It had gotten dark, only then did the outer temple complex come into view beyond the nearer roofs, its pale stone catching the afternoon light. A satellite sanctuary, subordinate to the central temple deeper within the city but vital in its own right.

Its walls stood open, wide enough for passage and thick enough to hold. Bells chimed somewhere within, steady and unhurried.

He paused at the threshold as a group of students crossed the courtyard ahead of him, robed, orderly, and quiet. Instinctively, he stepped aside to give them space.

One person moved against the flow. She kept to the edge of the courtyard rather than passing through it, close to the stone near the colonnade. Smaller than many around her, she carried herself straight despite the worn leather satchel at her side. Her hair was pulled back neatly, dark against the pale fabric of her robes, practical rather than ceremonial. She moved with care shaped by habit.

She noticed him at the same moment he noticed her. She stopped. For a heartbeat, neither spoke.

His stance was careful rather than ready, his weight steady as though unsure how much space he was permitted to take. He was broader than most, built for endurance rather than display, yet he carried it without confidence, posture guarded. His features were sharper than those of the temple-born, weathered by sun and travel rather than sheltered study.

The wooden shield at his back was worn but well kept, its edges marked by use. His hands bore the signs of training, callused and steady, close to his chest as they gripped the straps of what he carried.

"Are you lost?" she asked. Her voice was calm, neutral. Polite without warmth or distance.

"No," Thall replied after a brief pause. "Just arriving."

She nodded once. "The administrative hall is to the east. Visitors are expected to report there first."

"I will," he said. After a moment, he added, "Thank you."

She turned to leave, then paused long enough to look back. Her gaze moved briefly to his hair, lighter than was common here, then to the sun-darkened skin of his hands.

"You're from Eldhar," she said quietly.

"Yes." He nodded again.

"Temple rules still apply," she said. "Even to visitors."

"Of course," Thall replied.

"I'm Sakura," she said, as if the name were part of the transaction.

"Thall," he replied.

She inclined her head and continued on.

Thall watched her walk away.

Inside the administrative hall, he waited longer than expected on a narrow stone bench while messages were reviewed, seals inspected, and instructions delayed behind procedure.

At last, the clerk returned and spoke without looking up. "Not today," he said. "Come back at first bell."

Thall inclined his head, stood, and turned away. The delay pressed against his patience, restrained by habit. By the time he stepped back into the courtyard, evening had begun to gather. He nearly collided with someone moving the other way.

Sakura caught herself first, one hand bracing against the stone pillar beside him.

"Apologies," Thall said.

She inclined her head once. "Thall."

He returned it.

She slid the satchel higher against her hip and tightened the strap.

"You'll want the west path if you're leaving tonight. The eastern road closes after sunset."

"They told me to come back at first bell." he said.

She studied him again. "Then you'll need lodging approval."

He nodded.

"There's a clerk assigned to evening intake," she said. "Come with me." She started walking before he had the chance to answer.

They moved through narrower corridors together, past study chambers and garden courtyards. Sakura spoke only when necessary, her directions precise and unambiguous.

After a stretch of silence, Thall asked, "Have you been here long?"

"Long enough to know where not to be late." she said.

He smiled faintly. "That sounds familiar."

She glanced at him. "Does it?"

"Yes," he said.

They reached a small office tucked behind the main records hall. Sakura spoke quietly to the clerk inside. He listened, checked a ledger, then nodded once. A rate was recorded, a stamp pressed into place, and a key slid across the desk.

"There," she said, handing it to him. "It's modest, but it's clean. Payment is due in the morning."

"That's fine," he replied. He accepted the key and tucked it away.

She turned to leave, then paused. "You watch carefully," she said. "That doesn't come from comfort."

Thall considered that. "Maybe," he replied. "Or maybe it's learned."

She allowed a brief smile. "Good evening, Thall."

"Good evening, Sakura," he replied.

She walked away into the fading light.

Thall turned toward the lodging hall.

Chapter 14: Echo Of First Bell

The market in Hanzhong never truly slept.

Thall crossed the temple grounds before the bells were rung. The clerk who met him listened, checked his seal, and sent him on with a nod. "After first bell," he said.

By the time Thall reached the outer square, the city had begun to stir in earnest. Vendors called prices, carts rolled over stone, and voices carried news alongside goods. He moved through it with one hand near the strap of his pack, eyes alert.

He had not intended to linger, but returning to Serenthall without a small token from Hanzhong sat poorly with him.

He passed a produce stall set close to the lane. The baskets were fuller than he was used to, roots thick and clean, greens stacked high without wilt. The air carried a scent that cut through the dust—fresh, sharp, and warm at once. He slowed without meaning to, then moved on.

Near a stall of carved wood and dyed cloth, he slowed. Something small and useful. He reached the end of the row and turned back.

Nearby, another cloth merchant leaned toward a neighboring vendor, his voice pitched low but carrying just enough to be overheard.

"...Dominion made an example of him," the merchant murmured. "Public square, at first bell."

Thall slowed. "Who?" he asked.

The merchant glanced at him, irritation flickering across his face. "This doesn't concern you." His gaze lingered, taking in Thall's clothes, his bearing. "You're not from here."

"Who," Thall asked again.

The merchant hesitated. "A weaver," he said. "Lower streets. Thought he could act against the Dominion without being seen."

"Berrin," Thall said.

The merchant frowned. "That was the name." He reached beneath the stall and drew out a scrap of parchment, torn from a wall and folded once. "Posted at dawn."

Thall took it.

The notice was brief and official, the ink still dark. Berrin's name stood in neat script. Below it, another line marked the time: first bell.

"There was another name." The merchant said.

Thall's grip tightened. The parchment dipped in his hands.

"Eldrin," he said.

"Him," the merchant replied. "Same place."

Thall lowered his eyes.

The words did not arrange themselves at once. Meaning came all at once, too much and without order. He stood where he was as the market moved around him, the space suddenly vast, the paths away too narrow to matter.

"It can't be." He mumbled.

His footing failed.

He took a step that did not land where he expected. The parchment crumpled as his fingers gave way. His vision narrowed.

Darkness came.

◆ ◆ ◆

He woke to quiet. Not the quiet of the road or the square, but the stillness of clean air and cool stone. A pale ceiling rose above him. Bells chimed slow and steady, close enough to feel.

He tried to sit up.

"Easy," a voice said.

Hands pressed at his shoulder, firm.

Something cool touched his forehead. A damp cloth, faintly scented with herbs.

He blinked. Dark hair pulled back. Eyes already focused.

"You collapsed," Sakura said. "A merchant brought you in."

"I have to go," he said, pushing against the pressure.

"Not yet."

There was no room in her voice for argument.

Another presence moved in close. A student assistant he did not recognize steadied him as his strength wavered.

Sakura kept the cloth in place.

The bells sounded again.

Thall's breath hitched. His eyes found hers.

"First bell."

"It has already passed," she said.

The words reached him slowly.

A sound broke from him. His body folded forward, strength leaving all at once. His hands clenched at his chest, then fell away.

Sakura moved with him, one arm bracing his shoulders as another set of hands joined hers. They propped him upright until his breathing steadied.

She stayed without speaking. When the shaking eased, she set the torn notice flat on the small stone table beside the bed and straightened.

She hesitated, then turned away. The assistant followed, their footsteps fading until the room returned to stillness.

Thall remained seated, feet flat against the stone. He waited until the weakness drained from his limbs and his breath slowed.

The parchment lay where Sakura had left it.

He glanced at it but did not touch it.

When he stood, it was without hurry. He gathered his pack, adjusted the strap across his shoulder, and left the ward.

He did not return to the room.

The tavern on the western lane was loud enough to keep distance between him and the quiet. He took a seat near the back, where the light thinned. No one paid him much attention.

He came back the next night.

And the one after that.

Always the same corner. Always facing the room. He kept his drink close and his words to himself. When others laughed or argued, he stayed apart from it. The tavern maid learned to leave him undisturbed, setting the cup down when it emptied.

Later that week, he stood and left while the place was still loud.

His room was as he had left it. Spare and quiet. He set his pack on the table and sat across from it without removing his cloak.

After a time, he reached inside and drew out the map.

He unfolded it slowly, smoothing the creases. Serenthall lay where it always had.

His hand rested elsewhere, still and deliberate, as if waiting for something to answer.

Chapter 15: The Search

There was little to take that had belonged to her at all. Only her birth parchment, folded thin from years of careful keeping, its edges softened by handling.

The decision had already been made by the time the bell marked the final watch. She waited until the halls fell into shallow, uneasy sleep, until the passageways emptied and the wind carried only the sound of the sea against stone.

She paused once at the threshold of the dormitory, her fingers brushing the worn edge of the frame.

The keepsake lay hidden beneath her collar, warm against her skin. Proof she had not imagined what she had seen. Proof that the rules she had been taught were incomplete.

Lea stepped into the night and did not look back.

On the upper floor of the orphanage, in a narrow office lit by a single lamp, Instructor Grey stood at the window. He watched her slip through the outer gate without comment, his reflection faint against the glass. When she was gone from sight, he turned away. Some lessons could not be taught by keeping someone inside.

The road away from Aegis Enclave was narrow and poorly marked, winding between stone and scrub before giving way to open ground. Lea traveled lightly, avoiding lantern-lit paths and stopping only where the terrain allowed clear sight in every direction.

She had not left empty-handed. The orphanage kitchens were never locked, only observed through habit and expectation, and she took what would not be missed. A waterskin, dry bread wrapped in cloth, a small bundle of preserved fruit. Enough to last if she moved with care.

The books had been harder to take, not because they were guarded, but because they had been left where curiosity was expected to fail. She retrieved them from the upper shelves of the library, cracked spines and crowded margins marking them as references rather than instruction. She was quick and deliberate, taking only what she meant to commit to memory.

She walked until the ache could no longer be ignored, then rested where stone rose close at her back and the wind carried sound cleanly.

She never read for long. By moonlight, she sometimes summoned a small arcane orb, no brighter than a candle, and kept it low while she read. She paused between passages, dimming the light when it traveled too far, closing the book at the first change in the dark.

Once, wings passed overhead, the air disturbed just long enough to notice before the sound was gone. By dawn, she committed what she could to memory and moved on again.

◆ ◆ ◆

At sunrise, a bird perched on a low branch near where she had stopped, close enough that she could hear the soft adjustment of its weight. Its feathers caught the light, and it did not draw back.

"Are you following me," she said.

Lea did not reach for it or tense. She exhaled and continued reading, aware of its presence in the same quiet way she was aware of her own breath.

When she turned the page, the bird remained.

She gathered her things more slowly than before, exhaustion pressing into her stride.

A dull thud reached her through the trees. Then another. The ground answering the weight of hooves. A low neigh followed, distant but near enough to pull her attention.

Lea hesitated, then moved toward the sound, pushing through a narrow break in the brush where the ground sloped open.

Beyond the clearing, a skymare stood at the far edge of the field. Her white coat caught the light, her mane a deep red along her neck. Her wings were folded tight against her flanks; feathers pale near the body and darkening to red toward the outer edges. She did not flee when Lea stopped. One ear angled forward. Her breathing stayed slow and even.

Lea remained where she was. Her gaze moved once from the skymare to the bird perched nearby, then back again. She inclined her head a fraction in acknowledgment and let her attention pass forward. The distance between them did not close.

She slowed at the edge of the clearing, her steps shortening as fatigue caught up with her.

The skymare stood where the field opened, her white coat catching the light, wings folded tight against her flanks. She did not flee when Lea stopped. She watched her instead, calm and assessing, her attention fixed without tension.

Lea stepped forward once, then stopped well short.

Her hands stayed low by her sides. She resisted the instinct to shape, to answer the presence pressing faintly against her chest. She remained still, making no attempt to close the distance between them.

The skymare's wings mantled once, then eased back into place. She lowered her head slightly and raised it again, her gaze steady.

Wind moved through the grass. Lea's breathing slowed until it matched the rhythm around her.

After a span she could not track, the skymare stepped closer, closing part of the distance by her own choosing.

"Scarlet," Lea said quietly, the name offered without intent.

The skymare inclined her head once.

Lea exhaled, slow and deliberate, letting the tightness ease from her chest. She stayed where she was, allowing the moment to pass without pursuit.

Light continued to rise across the field.

◆ ◆ ◆

Then awareness pressed in, distinct from sound or motion. Lea steadied her breathing and let her attention extend outward, following the edge of the unease without giving it shape.

"You can relax," a voice said, calm and certain. "If I wanted your pack, you would not still be standing."

Lea hesitated.

A man stood just beyond the edge of the clearing. His posture was easy but balanced, his attention on her rather than the hound at his side.

"Thorne," he said. "Faunacre. Bramble Clan."

He tipped his chin slightly toward the hound. "My girl, Ashe."

"Lea," she replied after a brief pause. "Aegis Enclave."

Thorne's gaze moved past her, tracking the pale shape at the field's edge. His expression sharpened with interest.

"A skymare," he said. "You don't see them often." He paused. "You should put a lead on her. Leaving one loose draws attention."

Lea lifted her hand partway, then stopped. "I don't have a lead."

Thorne regarded her a moment longer, then nodded once, already turning away. "Wait here. I have one at camp. I'll bring it."

Lea turned back, glancing where the bird stood, but it was gone.

Farther back, a thin line of smoke rose from a cooking fire kept low against the stone.

He returned a short while later, the sound of his steps reaching her before he did. A length of braided leather hung from his hand, worn smooth by use.

He stopped a few paces away and extended it toward her.

"How much," she asked, keeping her voice level.

Thorne looked at her, then shook his head.

"No price," he said. His gaze drifted past her to the field beyond. Scarlet stood where she had been, pale against the rising light, watchful. "It's enough that I got to see her."

Lea followed his look. The lead rested loose in her hand.

"Thank you," she said.

She crossed the field at an unhurried pace, her steps even. Scarlet watched her approach without tension, stance unchanged.

Lea stopped within reach and waited. When the skymare did not turn away, she lifted the lead and set it gently around her neck.

Scarlet did not resist.

Thorne watched a moment longer. "You could have performed the bond," he said, not accusing.

Lea's hands remained steady. She drew a breath before answering.

"I don't have the capacity for that," she said.

Thorne studied her, then gave a small nod, accepting the answer as it stood.

Lea lowered her hand and stepped back, leaving the line slack between them.

Thorne inclined his head slightly, then stepped away, leaving the space between her and the skymare untouched.

"I was camped," he said, as if answering the question she had not asked. He nodded once toward the hound. "Ashe caught your scent. I came to see what had entered the clearing."

Ashe remained partly concealed by brush, head raised, eyes tracking Lea without tension.

"So... You've been watching me," Lea said.

"I was," he replied without apology. "I saw how you let her approach."

She studied him a moment, then inclined her head once. "You stayed back."

"Tamer's creed," he said.

She considered that, her gaze dropping briefly before returning to him.

He turned and walked back toward the fire. After a few steps, he stopped.

"You're not a thief," he said. "And you're not running."

"I'm not a thief," Lea replied without pause. "My time at the orphanage has concluded."

"Then you're welcome to share the fire," he said, and continued on.

Lea waited a moment before following, guiding Scarlet by the lead.

◆ ◆ ◆

Thorne crouched near the fire; one hand braced against his knee. He drew the meat farther from the flame, then straightened.

Lea approached and stopped well outside the fire's edge. The hound's ears flicked once.

"Traveling alone?" he asked.

She nodded, carefully.

His gaze moved once toward the mare, then returned to her. Recognition passed across his expression, quiet and unremarkable.

She watched him tend the meat with care. The smell reached her before she realized how long it had been since she had last tasted meat. Her stomach tightened.

He noticed and said nothing.

"You hunt for yourself," she said, trying to keep her voice even.

"And for trade," he replied. "Depends on the road." He glanced at her once, then back to the fire. "You're headed east."

"Guardian's Hollow," she said, her gaze returning briefly to the food.

A corner of his mouth lifted. "Same."

"I finished a contract nearby," he went on. "Didn't expect company this far out."

"Neither did I."

He lifted the meat from the fire, cut it cleanly in two, and offered her the larger portion without comment.

Lea hesitated. "I don't have much to trade."

Thorne looked at her. "You could lighten my load," he said, nodding toward Scarlet.

After a moment's consideration, she accepted.

The hound's tail tapped the ground once.

They ate in silence, the fire snapping low between them. When Lea rose, it was not to prepare for travel, but to stand near Scarlet, resting her hand briefly at the base of her neck before stepping back again.

Thorne watched without staring. "You handle her with care," he said. "You don't rush her, nor give her more than she could take."

"Would you?" she asked, not expecting an answer.

That earned a real smile. "We'll reach the Hollow by nightfall if we don't hurry."

Lea glanced toward the road ahead, then back at the fire. "That works."

They traveled without haste. Thorne kept a steady pace, Ashe stayed close by his side; Lea matched him without effort, leading scarlet behind her.

❖ ❖ ❖

When the ground firmed beneath their feet and the road widened into packed stone, Guardian's Hollow announced itself.

The walls came first, then the watchtowers, then the smell of iron and beasts kept too long behind gates.

At the outer checkpoint, Thorne slowed rather than stepping ahead. One of the guards recognized him at once, his gaze moving from Thorne to Ashe.

"Thorne," the man said, more confirmation than greeting.

Thorne inclined his head.

The guard's attention widened to include Lea. Two guards flanked the gate, each with a sabretooth at their side. The beasts stirred, heavy heads lifting, eyes tracking Lea and the mare while their handlers watched in silence.

Scarlet drew her wings closer to her flanks.

The guards took a moment longer with her, reading posture and control rather than threat. Suspicion eased into assessment.

"Name," one of them said.

"Lea," she replied evenly. "From Aegis Enclave."

The man glanced once at Scarlet. No explanation was needed. He stepped aside.

"Don't wander," he said. "Find a posting."

Inside the walls, the Hollow opened into layered yards and narrow passages cut with purpose rather than care. Beasts paced behind iron gates, their movement controlled and contained. Handlers worked in silence, gestures brief, commands low.

Thorne slowed so she could take it in.

"Outer yards handle intake and transit," he said. "Inner rings are training and holding. Temple annex sits east. Work boards are kept there." He gestured as they passed, never pausing.

"Most people don't stay unassigned long," he added. "If you're useful, they find you."

Lea kept her hands still, her presence drawn inward. "I won't be staying," she said. "Only long enough to earn a bed and provisions."

Thorne nodded. "That's how it usually starts." After a moment, he added, "Staying only matters if the work does."

He glanced toward the lowering light filtering through the upper yards. "I haven't been here a week myself."

She followed his gaze, then looked away. "I will manage."

He studied her, rubbed his jaw once, then adjusted the strap of his pack. "You can come with me."

She hesitated, then fell into step beside him.

The clerk's station sat beneath a stone arch near the lower quarters, lanterns already lit. Thorne spoke briefly, low and familiar. A mark was made in a ledger, and a key slid across the counter.

Lea shook her head. "I can't—"

"You don't need to," Thorne said.

She stopped. "I don't have anything to trade."

"Then you'll pay me back," he replied, simple as that.

Her mouth opened, then closed again. Whatever refusal she had prepared found no place to stand.

Thorne inclined his head once. "Get settled," he said. "We can talk tomorrow."

He turned away. "Second floor," he added. "First door on the left."

He left her with the key still warm in her hand.

Scarlet stood beside her, wings folded close.

Guardian's Hollow continued its work around her, gates opening and closing without pause.

For the first time since leaving the Enclave, Lea did not feel alone.

Chapter 16: The Cost of Staying

Lea woke before the bell.

It took her a moment to register the difference. The ache she had come to expect was gone, replaced by a quiet steadiness that remained when she moved.

The room lay still. No voices in the corridor, no signal calling her to stand. Pale morning light filtered through the narrow window, soft and warm.

She sat up and waited, listening.

The Hollow was awake, but it did not press on her. Somewhere below, iron rang against stone. A beast shifted in its stall. An elemental hummed, low and contained, felt more than heard.

She dressed quickly, folding her blanket before she left.

The keepsake rested beneath her collar where she had placed it the night before. She checked it by habit, adjusted her cloak, and stepped into the corridor, leaving what had come before her behind, moving forward.

The stables lined the inner yard, cut partly into the rock. Cool air met her at the threshold, carrying the familiar scents of hay and leather. Scarlet stood where she had been left, wings folded close, her head lifting as Lea entered.

Lea stopped just inside the doorway.

She let her breathing slow and waited until Scarlet's weight evened. Only then did she step closer and rest her hand against the skymare's neck.

"That's good," Lea murmured, more to herself than the mare.

Footsteps sounded farther down the row, boots against stone. A voice carried between the stalls, calm and unhurried.

"...the route ran longer than expected."

She recognized it at once.

Lea inclined her head briefly toward the voice and returned her attention to Scarlet. A quiet touch at the skymare's shoulder was enough. Scarlet stepped forward, wings drawing closer as she followed.

"It often does," another voice replied, older, controlled. "But the threat won't return."

They moved together down the row at an even pace.

"Low pay," Thorne said, "but the ground was clean."

"Which means you chose well," the other answered. "The Hollow needs judgment more than speed."

Thorne stood near the archway with Ashe at his side, speaking with a broad-shouldered man whose posture carried authority without emphasis. The man's attention remained on Thorne, stance relaxed, hands loose at his sides.

Thorne noticed her before she reached them.

"Morning," he said, turning slightly. The word carried easy familiarity.

"Morning," Lea replied.

The other man's gaze flicked toward her, brief and assessing, then returned to Thorne.

"This is Lea," Thorne said. "The traveler from last night." He turned slightly. "Master Tamer Roland."

Roland's attention returned to her, more deliberate now. His eyes moved from her stance to the skymare at her side, then back again.

"The guards mentioned you," he said. It was not a question. "Said you brought your skymare in calm."

"Yes, sir," Lea replied.

He nodded once. "That matters." His gaze shifted past them toward the inner yards, already moving on. "I've got work waiting."

He turned to Thorne. "If you're taking contracts, post them clean. No shortcuts."

Thorne inclined his head. "Always."

Roland gave Lea a final look, then crossed the yard with purpose.

She watched him go, then looked back to Thorne. "I was going to ask you something."

He turned toward her.

"I mean to take a job," she said. "But I don't know which ones are worth the road."

Thorne studied her for a moment, then nodded. "That's fair." He gestured toward the covered boards set along the temple wall.

They walked together. Ashe fell in beside him without cue. Lea rested her hand briefly against Scarlet's shoulder with her lead at hand.

◆ ◆ ◆

At the boards, Thorne read first in silence. Notices were pinned in tight rows, ink dark and practical. Hunting work marked by range and quarry. Escort routes listed with terrain and threat. Deliveries noted by distance and discretion rather than haste.

"Distance," he said at last. "Then terrain. Pay comes after."

Lea followed his gaze across the postings, eyes moving from hunts to escort lines to quiet runs that asked for patience more than speed.

"Because pay lies," she said.

A corner of his mouth lifted. "Often enough."

She indicated a modest notice near the bottom.

Thorne read it once, then nodded. "Short route. Clean ground. Parcel run."

Lea weighed it. "Low risk."

"Low coin," he said.

She inclined her head. "I could do that."

"Yes," he agreed. After a moment, he added, "First job's easier with someone else."

She looked at him. "You don't have to."

"I know," he said. "I'm offering."

She paused, then inclined her head. "All right."

Thorne reached up and took the notice from the board. "We'll leave after midmorning."

Lea nodded. For the first time since arriving at the Hollow, she did not wait for the road to decide for her.

The route was short, the ground clean, the work exactly what it had promised to be. Thorne spoke easily as they traveled, pointing out where the soil softened and where the path narrowed, offering what he knew without instruction or expectation.

Lea found the exchanges easier than she had expected. By the time they turned back toward the Hollow, the road no longer felt shared out of necessity.

When the next request came in, Lea did not look elsewhere.

Thorne noticed and said nothing. The pairing worked. Ashe took point where the ground narrowed and danger announced itself early. Scarlet did the hauling, she kept distance at a steady pace, alert to changes in terrain and movement beyond the road.

Lea prepared with care, asked when she needed to, and trusted his judgment once they moved. Thorne found he worked better with someone who understood the weight of a decision and did not argue for the sake of hearing her own voice.

By the third posting, the coin weighed more heavily in her pouch and the boards no longer surprised her.

The notices no longer blurred together. Thorne read them with care, gauging terrain, distance, and time before adjusting their supplies.

Lea noticed the pattern forming; preparation replacing conversation, trust expressed through routine rather than words.

The roads grew harder, and they moved like people who had learned each other.

"You walk quieter now," Thorne said after a while.

Lea glanced down at her boots. "I'm trying not to waste them."

He nodded. "Most people don't realize they're loud until someone tells them."

"You noticed," she said.

"It's my work." After a moment, he added, "You listen better, too."

She smiled faintly. "You don't talk much,"

"If you have questions, ask."

She took a few steps ahead, then slowed. "I do."

The corner of his mouth lifted despite him.

She glanced back, a trace of a grin appearing. "Where are we?"

"Still moving."

She let out a quiet breath of laughter. He did not, but his shoulders eased.

She spoke more than she intended after that, only realizing how easily the words had come when the day was nearly done.

◆ ◆ ◆

They were returning from an owlbear hunt when they heard the waterfall, the steady rush cutting through the forest. Thorne followed the sound, eyes on the ground, and found a clearing where the water ran clean and the noise swallowed the woods around it.

They camped there, drawn by the water and the way the spray cooled the air. The constant rush masked their movements and anything else that might draw near.

Lea worked beside Scarlet, easing the straps loose and lifting the load from the skymare's back. Scarlet stood patient and steady, wings folded tight, her attention angled toward the trees.

Nearby, Ashe circled once, nose close to the ground, then settled with her body turned toward the clearing's edge.

The arrow came without warning.

It struck Thorne high in the shoulder, the force twisting him partway as pain flared sharp and immediate. He grunted but stayed upright, his hand already moving for his bow.

Ashe broke from the clearing at the same instant, a dark blur driving toward the trees where the shot had come from.

Another figure burst through the spray, sword raised, closing fast.

Thorne shifted aside, the blade cutting air where his ribs had been a breath earlier. Pain dragged at his arm as he brought the bow across his body by instinct, the wood shuddering as the sword struck hard against it.

A second sound cut through the roar of water.

The swordsman stiffened, then pitched forward as an arrow struck him high in the back. He fell without a sound.

Lea stood beyond him, bow already lowered, her attention snapping back to Thorne.

Across the clearing, Ashe drove the archer to ground, snapping and circling to keep him off balance. Thorne forced himself forward, jaw tight, and raised his bow with his uninjured arm.

He loosed once.

The arrow struck clean. The archer collapsed. Ashe pulled back as the body went still.

The clearing quieted, the waterfall the only sound left, along with Thorne's rough breathing.

◆ ◆ ◆

Lea crossed the ground at once, already reaching for him. Scarlet remained where she was, watchful, wings tight, eyes on the dark beyond the trees.

Thorne took two steps, then faltered. He caught himself against a tree, breath shortening, before sliding down until the ground met him.

Lea dropped beside him, knees biting into the dirt. Her hands found the arrow without hesitation. She set her grip through effort rather than calm.

"Stay with me," she said, and pulled.

His body locked. The sound that tore from him forced its way through clenched teeth as the shaft came free. His head struck the bark behind him, breath breaking apart, each pull shallower than the last.

Lea pressed her palm to the wound at once, then reached for the satchel at her side, fingers shaking as they searched for cloth.

"Something's wrong," Thorne said. His voice thinned with strain.

She drew her hand back.

The blood had thickened, dark and wrong, clinging instead of flowing.

Lea stared. Her breath caught once before she could stop it. "That's not right."

Thorne forced his eyes open and followed her gaze. Understanding crossed his face.

"Venom," he said. The word dragged out of him. "Snake work."

Lea tore through the satchel, pulling vials free, then wraps, then nothing that mattered. Items dropped into the dirt unnoticed.

"I don't have anything for venom," she said. Her voice broke. "Nothing that can stop it."

She looked at him again, fear bare now. "Do you?"

Thorne shook his head.

Her hands moved faster, frantic now, searching again as if something might appear if she tried hard enough. "There has to be something," she said. "There has to be."

Ashe paced in a tight circle nearby, nails scraping stone, ears pinned as she lifted her head and whined low.

Lea's vision blurred, tears breaking free despite her effort to hold them back.

The pain dulled in his shoulder, spreading outward, heavy and distant. Thorne reached for her hands and caught them, his grip weak but deliberate.

"Lea," he said quietly.

She froze at the sound of her name.

"That's how it works," he said.

Her eyes filled. She swallowed and failed to steady herself.

"No," she said. The word broke as it left her. "You're still here."

He shook his head once. "It's too late."

Ashe stepped in close and pressed her muzzle to his cheek, tongue brushing his skin as she whined softly. She stayed there, breathing against him.

Thorne's breathing grew uneven; each pull shorter than the last. He looked at Lea as though keeping his head upright cost him effort.

"Take care of her," he said, barely audible. "She listens to you."

Lea shook her head, sharp and helpless.

Thorne's gaze dropped to Ashe. He lifted his hand with what strength remained and brushed his fingers along her cheek. His mouth curved, faint but real.

"She's good," he murmured.

Ashe pressed closer, whining low.

Thorne's hand dropped free and struck the ground.

The waterfall continued on.

Chapter 17: The Burden

Scarlet carried the owlbear across her back, wings folded tight as she moved ahead. Behind her, Lea had built a rough bier from branches and a cloak, the weight kept low to spare him. Thorne lay secured within it, wrapped and bound so his body would not strike stone or root. The knots were neat. Her hands had done that part without instruction.

Lea walked beside the bier, close enough to steady the load if it shifted, close enough that even a single step of distance felt wrong. Branches whispered and scraped along the ground as they moved.

Ashe paced back and forth, unable to choose where she belonged. Her ears lifted again and again at sounds that never followed. She nosed the road, the brush, the air, searching as though the right scent or motion might still undo what had already happened.

The road to Guardian's Hollow stretched longer than it should have. Silence did that. It forced every step to matter. Lea did not try to fill it.

Her pack weighed less than it should have. The bandages were gone. So were the tinctures she had rationed since leaving the Enclave. Dried blood darkened the cuffs of her sleeves where she had wiped her hands and forgotten.

Now there was only getting him back. Guardian's Hollow did not leave its dead on the road.

The outer watch path came into view near dusk, cut into the rise above the road.

Lea did not lift her head.

The guards stepped forward as Scarlet approached, the sabretooth beasts at their sides rising together. One of the beasts went taut and turned toward Ashe.

"That's... Thorne," one guard said quietly.

Lea nodded slowly.

The second guard's gaze moved to the bier behind Scarlet, then away. His jaw set.

The gate opened without a word.

Inside, the Hollow heads turned, and voices lowered. A woman leading a tethered beast paused and stepped aside as Scarlet passed beneath the weight. A boy carrying a water pail stopped until his mother drew him gently away.

No one reached for Lea or tried to comfort her. They simply cleared space. Then the hollow continued.

She walked toward the low building near the training yard, plain and functional. She recognized it by scent before she reached the door. Clean linen, bitter herbs, and beneath it all the old trace of blood that never left the wood. The place never stayed quiet for long.

An assistant met them at the threshold and halted when he saw the bier. "Keeper Harlan," he said softly.

Harlan stepped forward older than most, grey threaded through his hair. He recognized the body across the bier and moved at once, signaling for help.

The men approached Scarlet with care. Scarlet held still, eyes wide, her weight locked through her frame.

"I'll do it," Lea said, stepping forward. The words came sharper than she intended.

Her hands went to the knots. She loosened the rope, freed the cloak, and guided the weight down with a slowness that felt cruel. Two men took Thorne's shoulders and legs, lifting him as gently as they could before carrying him inside.

◆ ◆ ◆

Keeper Harlan watched without comment. When the body was set upon the cold slab, he nodded once.

"We have him."

The room held only what was required: a table, a basin, shelves lined with jars. The Hollow's tamers did not decorate.

They drew the cloak back.

Harlan's gaze went to the shoulder at once. The blood there had darkened and thickened, clinging where it should not have. He did not touch it.

"Snake poison," he said.

Lea nodded. "From an arrow."

Her eyes moved to Thorne's face. The strain that had shaped it before was gone, stripped away, leaving a stillness untouched by breath or pain. Darkened streaks marked his collar. His hands lay unmoving.

Ashe padded into the room and stopped short. She lowered her head and nosed Thorne's fingers, then gave a thin, broken sound. Her tail hung without motion.

Lea reached out, then stopped.

Her hands hovered, uncertain.

Harlan watched her for a moment, then turned to the others. "Prepare him."

No words needed to be spoken, only the quiet work of washing him and wrapping him before moving on. Duty did not pause for death in Guardian's Hollow, but neither did respect.

Lea stood against the wall while they worked.

They removed his armor piece by piece and set it aside.

When they finished, one of helpers paused and reached for the seam at Thorne's shoulder. He worked the stitching loose with careful fingers and lifted free the Bramble clan patch, darkened by age and wear.

He crossed the room and placed the bundle in Lea's hand.

She closed her fingers around the cloth without looking down.

Harlan met her eyes. "You came back," he said.

Lea inclined her head once.

"Where are you headed now?" he asked. The question carried no pressure.

Lea opened her mouth and found nothing there.

Ashe pressed more firmly against her leg, steady and insistent. Outside the doorway, Scarlet waited with her head lowered and wings tucked, shifting her weight.

"I don't know," Lea said.

Harlan regarded her a moment longer, then inclined his head and turned back toward the table.

Lea did not argue. She turned to leave, one hand resting at Ashe's collar, her steps careful as she reached the doorway.

Roland nearly collided with her.

He halted at once, his eyes moving from her face to the room beyond her. Whatever he had been told settled into certainty. He removed his hat, pressed it to his chest, and stepped inside.

"I'm glad you made it back," he said quietly.

Lea inclined her head.

"I'll send word to the Bramble clan," Roland went on. "By bird. They'll know before nightfall."

She stepped aside without speaking. Roland passed her and moved deeper into the room, already turning toward Harlan as Lea guided Ashe down the corridor.

At the outer yard, Lea turned toward the posting hall to close out the owlbear contract. Ashe stayed close by her side.

Scarlet followed with the lead dangling, wings tucked, keeping pace.

Chapter 18: Loose Threads

Earlier that afternoon, at the heart of the Lianhua Dynasty in the city of Hanzhong, the central temple halls lay quiet.

Sakura stood before High-Priest Liang, posture straight, expression composed. The scroll on the table had already been stamped.

Liang regarded her a moment. "Your work in the healing practice exceeded my expectations," he said. "The results were noted."

Sakura inclined her head. "Yes, Lead Priest."

Liang then picked up the document.

"You are needed elsewhere," he continued, placing the document into her hands.

She accepted it without comment.

"This assignment will account for the remainder of your service," Liang said. "You have completed six months. Four and a half years remain."

"Where am I sent?" she asked.

Liang met her gaze. "Guardian's Hollow."

Sakura drew a measured breath. She had heard of Guardian's Hollow. "A difficult assignment."

"A necessary one," Liang replied. "They require steady hands and restraint."

He gathered the remaining papers. "Do not travel alone if it can be avoided. The roads between kingdoms are unkind to the unguarded."

Sakura inclined her head once. "I am sure to find someone."

Liang's expression softened slightly. "Before you leave, you will return home."

Sakura's breath caught before she could stop it. She inclined her head. "Yes."

When dismissed, she hurried to her room, getting ready her smile not leaving her.

She left Hanzhong with her satchel light. By the time she reached the path leading toward Zhìyé and the fields beyond, the sun was already lowering. Her pace lengthened without conscious choice.

◆ ◆ ◆

Her mother's house stood close to the land. Mira was in the fields when Sakura arrived, moving steadily between the rows, sleeves rolled, posture sure.

Mira looked up and froze for a heartbeat. Then she crossed the distance quickly and drew Sakura into a brief embrace before pulling back.

Behind them, Anya stood in the doorway. Tears slipped free without restraint, one hand braced against the frame as she watched.

"You're home," Anya said.

Sakura turned to her at once and stepped into an embrace that held. She said nothing as they moved inside together, Anya's hands rising to her shoulders as they passed through the doorway.

Mira followed a moment later, wiping her hands on her trousers before closing the door behind them.

They gathered around the table. Anya took the chair near the hearth. Mira sat opposite her, hands folded, watching. Sakura remained standing until her mother reached for her wrist, then she sat as well.

Anya studied her closely. "They sent you back?"

"For a day," Sakura said. "Before my next assignment."

Anya let her breath out slowly and nodded once. "Then we'll make the most of it."

Sakura reached across the table and took her mother's hands. They were warm and rough from work, the skin worn thin beneath her fingers. Anya's posture stayed upright by habit, though the effort in the way she breathed.

"You look tired," Sakura said quietly.

Anya gave a small shake of her head. "That comes with the land."

Mira said nothing. She watched from across the table, hands folded, her gaze moving between them.

Sakura released her mother's hands and reached into her satchel. She set a small, stoppered vial on the table, the liquid inside dark and fragrant.

"This is for you," she said. "You should drink it."

Anya frowned faintly and did not reach for it at once. "That sort of thing isn't cheap."

"I grew the herbs myself," Sakura said. "I brewed it too. And that lowered the cost"

She stepped behind her mother and placed a hand lightly between her shoulders. "This will help your lungs," she said. "Drink all of it."

Anya hesitated, then lifted the vial and drank. She set it back on the table and stayed very still.

Sakura kept her hand where it was and spoke the incantation, low and steady. The incantation used the elixir as conduit, mending the weary bones and lingering aches that had burdened her mother for years.

Anya drew a deep breath, then another. Her shoulders lowered as the air filled her lungs. She leaned back and closed her eyes briefly. When she opened them again, she reached up and covered Sakura's hand with her own, holding it there, firm and certain.

Only then did Sakura let her own breath out.

She crossed to where Mira sat near the hearth.

Mira looked up at once.

"You're not late to school anymore," Sakura said with a warm smile.

Mira blinked. "I—" She let out a breath that nearly laughed. "I suppose we solved that."

"You did more than that," Sakura said.

She reached into her satchel and drew out a small coin pouch, worn but kept with care. It gave a familiar sound when she placed it in Mira's hands.

Mira stiffened. "Sakura—"

"You earned it," Sakura said, her voice firm now. "Every morning you ran from the fields to the basin. Every lesson you missed so I could stay. Every time you said it was fine."

Mira stared at the pouch as though it might disappear. Her fingers tightened around the cord.

"I didn't do it for this," she said, her voice breaking.

"I know," Sakura replied. "That's why it matters."

Mira's shoulders shook once. She clutched the pouch to her chest, then stood unsteadily and pulled Sakura into a fierce embrace that left no space for words.

Sakura held her just as tightly.

Behind them, Anya watched in silence with one hand covering her mouth.

After a moment, Anya lowered her hand and turned back toward the hearth. Mira followed without speaking and sat beside her.

They ate as the light faded. When the fire burned low, they were still talking, first of small things, then of stories that had waited years for the right moment. Somewhere past midnight, words gave way to quiet. They slept where they sat, warmed by the hearth and by the rare certainty of being together, if only for a night.

◆ ◆ ◆

Morning came softly.

Anya woke first. She sat for a time, testing her breath and her joints, the steadiness that had carried through the night. Only then did she reach out and touch Sakura's cheek, as if to confirm she was there.

"You should go soon," Anya said gently. "While the light is good."

Sakura opened her eyes and caught her mother's hand. She drew the cover Anya had placed over her in the night higher, and let out a long breath. "Just a little longer."

Anya nodded and let her rest.

Sakura stayed through the morning, until her mother's color steady and the household eased into its familiar rhythm.

When the time came, she gathered her satchel. Mira stepped forward first and held her in a brief, firm embrace. Neither of them spoke.

Anya followed, smoothing Sakura's hair back from her face as she had when she was little. "Travel steady," she said.

"I will be back," Sakura replied.

She stepped outside and closed the door behind her. For a moment, she rested against the wood, breathing until the tightness in her chest eased. Then she turned and began the walk back toward Hanzhong.

Inside the house, Mira returned to the table and sat, the pouch in her hand. After a long moment, she loosened the cord. Lamplight caught on gold, not copper or silver, it was enough to carry them through winter and beyond. Mira closed her hand around the coins, a single tear escaping.

By the time Sakura reached the temple grounds, lamps were being lit for the night.

She followed the outer walk to the small rented room she had helped secure for him. She paused outside the door, rested her hand briefly against the frame, and knocked once.

"Come in," he said after a moment.

She opened the door and stepped inside, leaving it open behind her.

Thall sat at the small table, an unfolded map spread beneath his hands. He leaned forward slightly, one finger tracing a road he did not intend to take yet. His shoulders were squared, his posture controlled.

Sakura paused and took that in.

"Forgive the intrusion," she said quietly.

He lifted his head. When he saw her, his eyes were tired but clear, as if sleep had come in pieces.

She glanced at the map in his hand. "Are you returning home?"

The question drew his full attention. He studied her as though only then noticing she had come with purpose.

"No," he said after a moment. "Not yet."

He folded the map once, then again, with care. "Why are you here?"

"I've been reassigned," she said. "Guardian's Hollow."

He considered it. "That isn't a posting for rest."

"It isn't optional," Sakura said. "I'm expected to serve."

He inclined his head slightly. "And you assumed I'd walk with you."

She met his eyes. "I assumed you'd know the road."

He was quiet for a beat. "I know roads like that."

She nodded once. "That will do."

He studied her. "And payment?"

"I'll receive two gold and ten silvers for travel," Sakura said. "Half is yours."

Thall set the folded map aside. "I'll go with you."

She nodded. "We leave at first light."

He drew back slightly. "I will be ready by morning," he said.

She left him then, returning to her room.

Sleep came unevenly, but it came.

◆ ◆ ◆

Thall woke before the light reached the floor.

The ache was there, dull and familiar, but it did not slow him. He gathered the few things he had left unpacked, folded the blanket once, and strapped his pack tight.

Key in hand, he stepped into the corridor and made his way toward the clerk's desk near the outer hall. The temple grounds were quiet, just beginning to stir. He placed the key on the counter and counted out the remaining coin for his stay, exact and unhurried.

The clerk nodded and slid the key away without comment.

Thall turned, adjusting the strap across his shoulder, and nearly crossed paths with Sakura as she came up the steps.

"Morning," she said.

"Morning." He inclined his head.

"I have coin for the road," she said, falling into step beside him as they walked. "Food, passage, whatever we need."

He paused, then nodded once. "I'll need my share now," he said. "Before we leave."

She reached into her satchel, counted it out, and placed his portion in his hand without hesitation.

Thall weighed it once in his palm, then nodded. "Good."

He turned toward the market path. "We should go while the stalls are still setting up. It would do us well to eat before we take the road."

They gathered bread and dried fruit, waterskins drawn and sealed. Enough to break their fast and carry them through the first stretch. What remained was taken without comment: herbs, cloth, bandages.

Thall added rope and whetstone.

When they finished, Sakura lifted her satchel and drew it over her shoulders. The weight pulled her forward slightly.

Thall watched, then stepped in without asking, to take the larger pack she had.

She paused. "You don't have to."

"I do," he said, tightening the last buckle.

When they were ready, they turned toward the road.

Not far beyond the gates, the path split. One route curved north, familiar and worn. The other bent south, longer and exposed. Thall took the southern road. Sakura followed without question.

As they passed the marker at the crossroads, Sakura glanced once at the sign pointing north. **Serenthall Village** was carved there; she said nothing and kept walking.

The land opened quickly. Fields gave way to rolling hills where wind moved freely and sound traveled farther than it should. There was no cover there, nowhere to disappear. Thall kept the lead and set the pace, easing his stride when Sakura began to lag so she could match him without noticing.

They pressed on, slowing only when Sakura asked for time to gather herbs she deemed necessary. In the open ground, every sound felt closer than it belonged.

The shouting reached them without warning, sharp with fear, followed by the sound of beasts.

Ahead, a carriage stood canted off the road, one wheel caught hard against stone. Two wild beasts circled a man scrambling backward in the dirt.

Thall dropped the packs before Sakura could speak.

"Stay back," he said, already moving.

She caught his arm for the span of a breath. "Wait." Then she set her hand between his shoulders and spoke the incantation, her voice low and even.

The response came at once. It moved through him without flare or heat, leaving his body lighter, his balance keen.

Chapter 19: Fire In the Heart

Thall drew his short sword as he closed the distance.

One of the beasts lunged, low and fast, jaws snapping where his leg had been a moment before. Thall stepped inside the reach instead of away from it, shoulder turning as the blade came across in a tight arc. The cut met less resistance than it should have, the body giving too easily as blood followed the strike, quick and dark.

The beast crashed into the dirt and did not rise.

The second circled wide, claws scraping stone as it tested the space between them. It feinted once, then again, snapping at air. Thall did not chase it. He stayed where he was, blade low, eyes fixed, letting the scent of blood carry.

The beast hesitated. Its ears flattened. Then it broke and fled into the brush, the sound of its passage tearing through undergrowth before fading.

The man lay on his back in the dirt, staring up at Thall, breath tearing in and out as though he had forgotten how to draw it properly.

"You alive?" Thall asked.

The man nodded. "Yes."

Sakura approached at once and knelt beside him, already checking for injuries. "Sit," she said. "Let me see."

He looked at her more closely, breath still rough. "Sakura," he said, recognition cutting through the strain.

She met his eyes and inclined her head once. "Corvin."

Thall turned away once she had him. He set his blade aside, righted the carriage wheel, and checked the harness straps in quick sequence. One of the pack animals had bolted, but the remaining horses held, breath hard, eyes rolling until the noise faded and the scent of blood thinned. Gradually, they eased.

He did not approach them. Instead, he stepped back toward the road, blade still in hand, watching while Sakura worked behind him.

"You're shaken," Sakura said. "But you'll recover." Her hand rested between Corvin's shoulders as she spoke the incantation, low and even.

Corvin inclined his head to her first. "My thanks."

After a deep breath, he looked past her to Thall. "My escort left me two days back. Took one look at the hills and decided the road wasn't worth it." He reached into his coat and drew out a small pouch. "I can pay if you'll see me safely to Guardian's Hollow."

Thall did not answer at once.

Sakura met his eyes. "A carriage would save time."

"Fine," he said.

He took the pouch, loosened the cord, and tipped half the coins into Sakura's hand before tying it shut again.

Thall took the front bench beside Corvin as the carriage set out, leaving Sakura room behind them. Corvin kept his attention on the road and spoke only when necessary. Thall watched the horizon, steady and alert.

Sakura rested with her pack at her side, eyes closed but posture attentive, listening even when she did not look awake.

◆ ◆ ◆

Around midday the road grew harder to read, the carriage slowed before Corvin brought it to a stop.

He did not rein in at once. The wheels creaked as the horses slowed, ears pinned forward. Sound carried ahead of them through the open ground, snarls layered over heavier impacts, brush tearing where nothing small could pass.

Sakura leaned forward from the back; one hand braced against the rail. Thall had already turned in his seat, eyes fixed on the rise ahead.

An owlbear drove into view through flattened grass, feathers dark along its flank, one foreclaw raking wide as it snapped at a hound locked near its shoulder. Another owlbear pressed the far side of the clearing, bulk turned inward, wings tight to its frame as barbed feathers burst from its back in short, violent volleys.

The hounds were already among them.

They circled low and close, some bleeding, some limping, spacing kept by instinct rather than panic. One darted in and fell back with a cry as feathers struck deep.

At their center, a larger hound stepped forward and stopped.
Broad through the chest, heavier than the others, a pale scar crossed one eye. He did not charge. He paused, reading the space rather than the prey.

Thall drew a slow breath. Corvin brought the carriage fully to rest.

The fight closed in hard and near.

The hounds split. Two drew the owlbears' attention while the others pressed in from the flanks. Teeth sank deep. One hound went down beneath a sweeping claw and did not rise. Another tore free dragging a ruined leg.

The owlbears roared, snapping and turning, but they were already being pulled apart.

Thall stepped down from the carriage. He set his feet and raised his shield, sword ready at his side. He did not advance. He did not retreat. He stayed where he was and watched.

Sakura remained in the carriage, still and alert. Corvin kept one hand on the reins and did not look away.

The larger hound did not join the rush. He moved only when the owlbears broke position, pressing in then, driving one toward the others with a low snap of his jaws. When the last owlbear fell, the hounds closed together.

It ended soon after.

Silence followed, broken only by heavy breathing and the sound of bodies dragged across the grass.

The larger hound lifted his head and looked directly at Thall.

Corvin's voice came low from the seat. "That one knows us. Do not step forward."

They regarded each other across the space between them.

Thall neither lifted his shield nor lowered it.

The hound's ears angled forward, taking in a deep breath. Then he lifted his head and gave a single howl, low and carrying, meant to be heard rather than answered.

The pack gathered, then took their dead with them, teeth and shoulders working together as they pulled the fallen into the trees. The wounded followed last. The larger hound lingered only long enough to look back once more before turning away.

Thall lowered his shield.

Corvin exhaled slowly and eased his grip on the reins. "I don't know if I'm lucky, or cursed."

Thall inclined his head once, and hopped back on before the carriage moved on.

They returned to the road, Corvin drove while Thall sat beside him, his attention moving easily between the path ahead and the hills beyond. When Corvin spoke, Thall answered without hesitation, brief and certain, as though the choices ahead had already begun to arrange themselves.

Sakura sat behind them with a small book open in her hands.

◆ ◆ ◆

They reached the outer approach to Guardian's Hollow shortly before midday. The training yards came into view first, open ground traced by worn paths and broken by low stone barriers. Beyond them stood the gate and its watch.

The guards were already alert as the carriage slowed. Two stepped forward while a pair of bound elementals paced at their sides, large and silent, eyes fixed on the newcomers. Corvin brought the carriage to a stop without being prompted.

He initiated the exchange. One of the guards recognized him at once and inclined his head, already stepping aside. Attention turned to the others.

Sakura stepped down first. Pale skin and dark hair marked her as foreign immediately. Thall followed, lighter-haired, marked by travel in a different way. Against the guards' uniform features, neither belonged. The contrast was immediate.

Before Sakura reached for her satchel, Thall stepped forward. "We're expected," he said evenly. "Assigned healer for the Hollow."

Sakura paused, then passed him the papers with a nod. He handed them over, posture steady, gaze forward.

The guard reviewed the documents with care before returning them. His attention lingered on Thall, reading bearing rather than appearance.

"Stay clear of the yards unless instructed," he said. "The temple is open."

They were waved through.

As they passed the gate, Sakura glanced at Thall. The corner of her mouth lifted almost imperceptibly. She said nothing, but he noticed all the same.

Once inside, Corvin halted the carriage and climbed down. "I won't forget this," he said simply, looking between them. "If either of you ever need me, Holt Trading Company will answer."

His gaze returned to Sakura. From his coat he drew a small, stamped token and placed it in her hand. The seal was clean and unmistakable.

"You're a healer," he said. "If you decide to open a practice, you'll need steady supply before reputation carries you." He nodded toward the mark. "Show that seal and you'll receive preferred rates. Herbs, instruments, transport. We take care of our own interests early."

Sakura looked down at the token, then inclined her head. "Thank you," she said.

Thall inclined his head.

Corvin gave a short nod in return and turned toward the trade quarter to see to his business.

Thall did not want to linger, he turned to Sakura.

"The healer's hall," Sakura said quietly, turning towards the temple.

The Hollow revealed itself in layers as they crossed the yards. Tamers moved with beasts at heel, commands carried without voice, corrections made through posture alone. Nearby, summoners worked in quiet parallel, marks traced in the air or along stone, their attention split between the creatures bound to them and the space those creatures occupied.

Discipline here was visible rather than imposed, carried by habit instead of threat. Thall took note and kept moving.

They reached the temple steps together and entered.

The air inside was cool and dim, candlelight steady along the walls. The passage opened into a broad entry hall where footsteps softened, and voices carried farther than intended.

A woman stood just beyond the threshold, uncertain where to go next. Beside her stood a skymare.

Sakura slowed and stepped toward her. "Excuse me," she said. "I'm looking for the head priest."

The woman turned. Her posture was relaxed, but her eyes carried a weariness that did not match it.

"I'm Sakura," she added. "A healer, here for reassignment."

For a moment, the woman only looked at her. "Lea," she said at last.

Sakura inclined her head. "Do you know the way?"

Lea's mouth tightened. "A healer," she said. "We could have used one earlier."

Thorne's name went unspoken, but it rested between the words.

Before Sakura could answer, Thall spoke. "She arrived as fast as the road allowed."

Lea's attention shifted to him. She studied his face, the way he stood. Then she looked away.

After a moment, she adjusted her pack and turned toward the doors leading back out. A large hound waited just beyond the threshold.

"You'll find the head priest through the inner halls," Lea said, not looking at either of them.

She crossed the threshold without another word, leading the skymare, while the hound falling into step at her side as she moved.

Sakura waited until Lea was out of sight before moving again. "Come on," she said quietly.

They went deeper into the temple. When they reached the first corridor, Thall glanced back once, watching Lea cross the yard toward the inn, her pace even.

Then he turned forward and followed Sakura, the temple closing around them.

Chapter 20: The Unbound Truth

Sakura moved through the temple toward the inner halls, Thall keeping pace at her side.

The temple in Guardian's Hollow did not resemble Hanzhong in feeling. Stone and candle smoke lingered the same, but the weight behind them differed. In Hanzhong, silence pressed inward, shaped by ritual and expectation. Here, footsteps faded for simpler reasons. People learned early which sounds carried, and which were better left behind.

They continued along the inner corridor until the clerk stationed outside the head priest's office lifted his gaze.

"Purpose?" he asked, his tone neutral.

"Sakura," she replied. "Healer, reassigned from Hanzhong."

He glanced down at the ledger, finger tracing a line before stopping. A brief pause followed, long enough for the name to register.

"You were expected," he said. "You arrived quickly. And you don't waste time."

The novice nodded once and stepped forward.

Thall stopped without prompting. He adjusted his pack higher on his shoulder and took position against the stone wall, close enough to register approaching steps, far enough not to intrude. This was not a space meant for him, and he understood the distinction.

The door stood ajar. The novice knocked once and waited.

"Head Priest," he said quietly. "The healer from Hanzhong has arrived."

Inside, the room was narrow and removed from the main flow. A desk faced the far wall, its surface layered with scrolls, bound ledgers, and sealed correspondence. Books filled the shelves along the stone, their spines worn from frequent use.

Behind the desk hung the banner of Aetherwind. A deep purple field framed a single horn at its center, ringed in silver lines that caught the light without warmth. The symbol marked authority drawn from structure and oversight, not belief.

An older lady worked through a stack of records, Head Priest Aika; sleeves rolled to her forearms. She pressed a stamp onto the page, set it aside, then lifted her eyes. "Yes?"

"Sakura," she said. "Reassigned from the central temple of the Lianhua Dynasty in Hanzhong."

Aika studied her a moment, then nodded once. "I've been notified," she said. "You'll work alongside Keeper Harlan. You both fall under temple authority. Coordination passes through Master Roland."

"Yes, Head Priest."

"Follow," she said. "No delays."

Head Priest Aika turned and stepped out. Sakura followed, keeping pace, her satchel light compared to the packs in the yards, but carried with care.

Thall straightened as she emerged into the hall and fell in beside her without comment, his stride matching hers without crowding.

They passed from the temple interior into open air. The yards beyond were already active. Tamers moved in lines while summoners worked nearby, shaping restrained elemental forms under close watch. Beasts paced behind iron gates, observed by handlers with calm eyes and steady hands.

Aika glanced briefly toward Thall. "You are the escort."

"Yes."

"Remain close," Aika said. "The Hollow does not reward wandering."

"Understood," Thall replied.

The path narrowed as they moved into a smaller adjoining section of the Hollow. Noise softened. Doors stood open to rooms scented with herbs and clean cloth, work already underway.

The building they approached was modest and well placed, set between the temple and the yard gates, near enough to reach without crossing intake traffic.

It stood quiet among the others.

A sign hung above the door, its lettering softened by time but still clear.

"This practice is yours to run," Aika said, stopping at the threshold. "It has been unused for some time. You will operate independently, within temple regulation."

Sakura inclined her head.

"You've completed half a year," she continued, eyes dropping briefly to the record in her hand. "Four and a half remain. Once finished, you'll receive a full healer's license, with independent work permitted."

"Yes." Sakura nodded.

"Treatment has been entered. Fees assessed according to schedule. A clerk will collect at first bell for the previous day."

"Coordination with the yards remains necessary," she added. "Beyond that, your judgment stands."

Aika stepped aside and let her pass.

Inside, the ground floor opened into a waiting space longer than it was wide. A partial wall extended from one side, shielding the treatment area without fully closing it off. Light fell unevenly across worn stone and fixtures left in place.

"You sent for me?" A man stood in the doorway, his attention already on Aika.

"I did," she said. "This is Sakura of Hanzhong."

The man nodded once. "I heard you were coming."

"This is Keeper Harlan," Aika said.

"I'll begin sending cases by first light," Harlan said. "Only those that won't draw the yards."

"The space isn't set yet," Sakura replied. "I arrived today."

Harlan took that in, his eyes moving once around the room before returning to her.

"Then thank you for coming when you did," he said. "I'm a Keeper, not a healer. It helps, but it isn't what you bring."

He inclined his head. "Do what you can. I'll stagger what comes your way."

He turned to leave, then paused when he noticed Thall.

His gaze moved past him to Sakura and back again.

"You're with her," Harlan said, assessing him quietly.

"Escort," Thall said. "Thall."

"Harlan," he replied, already glancing toward the yard. "Some of the injured won't make the walk. If you're taking work, guide them here. The temple will pay."

Thall inclined his head. "That works."

Harlan nodded as he left. The head priest followed, already absorbed elsewhere.

Footsteps sounded at the doorway.

A broad-shouldered man with iron-gray hair stood there without announcement. His build was spare and hardened by use, posture upright without rigidity. He stepped forward with intent.

"Roland," he said. "Master Tamer of the Hollow."

Sakura turned to face him.

"You're the healer." Roland said, not questioning.

"Yes." She replied.

"You don't enter the yards alone," Roland continued. "You don't touch a beast without a handler. And you don't pretend magic stands in for discipline."

"I heal what's injured," Sakura said. "Not what should have been prevented."

Roland studied her, then nodded once.

His attention shifted briefly to Thall before he left. "Keep your work close until you learn the ground."

Sakura set her satchel down and looked around. Dust lingered in the corners. The basin showed old stains but no cracks. The shelves had gone untouched for some time.

"It'll take time," she said.

Thall glanced toward the door. "I'll wait outside."

"Not yet," Sakura replied. She moved past him, eyes scanning the space. "Would you stay until I've checked the building?"

He gave a short nod and followed.

◆ ◆ ◆

They moved through the structure together.

Downstairs, the waiting area revealed its full length. The partial wall extended farther than it first appeared, screening the treatment space and offering privacy when needed. Along the side, a small rear door opened onto a walled strip of compacted earth, once tended, its borders lined with cultivation frames now waiting, and a beast holding leading to the streets.

Beyond the main room, two doorways opened into dusty chambers with cots, set aside for injuries that lingered.

Upstairs, five narrow rooms opened off a short hall ending at an open kitchen beneath the eaves, plain but serviceable, clean and unused. One room opened into a smaller adjoining space barely large enough for a desk and shelves. Sakura paused there.

"This will work," she said.

Thall agreed with a quiet nod.

As they returned downstairs, Sakura slowed near the counter.

"Thank you," she said. "For bringing me here safely."

Thall inclined his head. "I needed the coin. And the time."

She studied him for a moment. "Are you heading back?"

He shook his head once. "Not sure."

"It would feel empty, living here alone," Sakura said. "Take one of the remaining rooms upstairs."

He hesitated.

"It doesn't come with expectations," she added. "Those rooms will remain unused otherwise."

Thall considered, then nodded. "All right." He met her gaze. "When you need someone for heavier work, you have me."

Sakura's shoulders eased. "That's acceptable."

"I'll take the front room with the adjoining space," she said.

"Then I'll take one at the back."

They worked without discussion. Sakura scrubbed stone and sorted what remained. Thall hauled discarded cloth and carried water from the yard, steadying a shelf when it resisted and shifting to heavier work when her hands tired.

By late evening, the practice no longer felt neglected. It was not ready, but it was awake.

They ate simply and cleaned what little remained. When the light softened, Sakura stood at the top of the stairs and listened as the building grew still around them.

Outside, iron rang against stone. A beast roared somewhere beyond the walls.

That night, Sakura slept without fully undressing, her door locked, the key left in place.

Down the hall, Thall sat on the edge of his narrow bed and listened to the Hollow breathe.

He stayed because leaving meant silence again.

Chapter 21: The Collective

First light came quietly.

Sakura woke before the bell, as she always did on days when work mattered. The building lay still around her, the last of the night's cool lingering in the stone. For a moment, she remained where she was and listened, letting the quiet turn into something she could use.

She dressed quickly and moved through the adjoining room, placing her records where she could reach.

Downstairs, the practice waited, clean enough to function and ordered enough not to slow her hands.

Sakura paused at the top of the stairs.

Thall was already awake. He stood near the counter, checking his gear with efficient care, his movements spare and deliberate. When he looked up, there was no question in his expression, only readiness.

A brief smile escaped her. She watched him a moment longer than she meant to, then started down.

"Morning," he said.

"Morning," she replied, nodding once.

They did not linger. Sakura lit the lamps and checked the basin while Thall adjusted the sword at his side, a pouch set at his other hip, shield close enough to reach.

He stepped out briefly, following the posted signs toward Harlan's practice near the yards, where early movement had already begun.

He returned shortly with the first case.

The man could barely keep his posture, his arm bound tight against his chest, breath shallow with pain. Thall guided him in without hurry and set him onto the stool beside the table.

Sakura uncovered the injury, read the swelling with her hands, then guided the joint back into place with steady pressure. The man hissed once, then sagged as the pain broke.

"Breathe," she said, calm and even.

She bound the arm and gave her instructions.

By then, Thall had already turned away. Once the man could sit on his own, he was out the door again, following the flow back toward the yards. When Sakura finished washing her hands, the next patient was already being brought in.

"This will hurt," she said, low and level.

She set the ankle, bound it, and spoke incantation as needed. The tamer nodded once in thanks as the pain eased and led the man back out.

More cases came without pause. A deep gash along a calf was cleaned, stitched, and wrapped. Another arrived with a fever left for too long, the patient shivering despite the warmth of the room. Sakura examined them all, speaking incantation only when required.

She moved from one case to the next without rushing, allowing a rhythm to form. Notes were written cleanly, costs named plainly, payment accepted before she turned to the next. Her voice stayed level, her instructions brief. She did not spend words on apologies or reassurances.

Midmorning, Harlan appeared briefly at the door. He watched in silence, eyes tracking the rhythm of the room, then set a small, wrapped bundle at the edge of the counter.

"From the stall by the east path," he said. "You'll forget to eat otherwise."

He nodded once to Sakura, and moved on.

When the room cleared for a moment, Sakura ate standing at the counter, only enough to quiet the ache in her stomach. She wrapped the rest and set it aside before turning back as the next patient came through the door.

By the time the flow eased again, she no longer thought about the space itself. Her hands moved without hesitation, the shelves answered her reach, and the basin drained as it should.

She leaned back against the counter for a moment. Thall noticed and set a cup of water within reach without comment.

◆ ◆ ◆

Later in the early afternoon, when the flow from Harlan's practice slowed, Thall stepped outside with the intention of checking the board.

He slowed when he saw a familiar young woman crossing the yard.

He recognized her from the night before, the one who had stood just inside the temple and spoken a name without explanation. A hound walked at her side, alert but with her tail low, head down. A skymare followed a few paces behind, wings folded tight against her body.

Thall watched long enough to know she was heading for the board, then turned toward it himself.

He arrived first. She joined him a moment later.

They stood near each other without speaking, reading the board in silence. Notices were pinned in tight rows, dark and practical ink. Escort work listed by route and threat level, deliveries judged by discretion rather than speed.

Thall broke the quiet. "First time taking from this board."

She glanced at him, studying him with the same steady attention she had shown the night before. "Don't start with distance," she said.

She lifted a finger and tapped the lower portion of the board, where the notices were shorter and more tightly written.

"That one," she added. "Short escort near the east road."

He read it carefully, slower than before.

"You're not taking it?" he asked.

She shook her head. "It doesn't suit me."

He nodded, then marked the posting.

"Thank you," he said.

That earned him a gentle nod.

"Lea," she said. "Ashe, and Scarlet." She indicated each in turn.

Ashe lifted her head at the sound of her name. Scarlet flicked an ear and stepped forward, closing the space toward Thall with ease rather than caution.

"Thall," he replied gently patting Scarlet on the neck, then turned and walked away.

Lea watched him go, then continued on, Ashe and Scarlet keeping pace.

"You like him," she murmured to Scarlet, not expecting an answer.

The job was quick, and the return was quicker.

Thall reported the completed escort to the temple clerk, accepted payment, and left before the ink fully set.

When he reached the practice, the door stood open.

He entered as an injured tamer was being guided out, arm newly wrapped, posture already lighter. Sakura stood at the counter, finishing her notes, hands steady.

"How did it go?" she asked, without looking up.

"Took a short job," Thall said. "No trouble."

She nodded and closed the ledger. "Good."

He set his sword aside within reach and leaned lightly against the wall. "I ran into Lea at the board."

Sakura looked up. "Lea?"

"The woman from last night."

"She helped me choose the job," he added. "Short route. Right call."

Before Sakura could answer, the door opened again.

A younger tamer entered too fast, breath uneven, attention fixed on what he carried. A young lion, mane not fully grown, lay cradled against his chest, body slack, one flank dark with blood.

"Please," the tamer said, his voice breaking. "Help."

"He clipped the ridge," he continued. "The wind pushed him into stone."

Sakura guided him to the back table. She eased the lion down, her hands reading the damage before her eyes finished taking it in. The wound was deep, the bleeding slow and persistent.

The tamer froze beside the table, hands hovering. "He's all I've got," he said, barely audible.

Sakura did not answer. She worked.

She cleaned the wound, pressed herbs into place, and watched how the lion responded. The bleeding slowed, but the breathing remained uneven.

Only then did she speak the incantation. Her voice stayed low and deliberate, shaped by intent rather than urgency, brief and controlled, placed with the same care as her hands.

Warmth gathered beneath her palms. The lion's chest rose more evenly. One paw flexed, claws scraping softly against the table before easing loose.

The tamer sank beside him, both hands buried in the mane. His breath broke, relief spilling out in quiet, unguarded sobs he did not try to stop.

Thall and Sakura stood back, watching in silence.

When Sakura stepped away, she washed her hands and spoke evenly. "He'll live. Keep him still for a few days. No training, and no work."

The tamer nodded, gathered the young lion carefully, and left without lingering.

The room stayed quiet for a brief moment.

◆ ◆ ◆

The practice sat quiet until the door opened again.

Lea stepped inside with Ashe at her side. She slowed just enough to take in the light and the order of the space, then fixed her attention on Sakura.

"You were late," Lea said.

The words landed flat at first.

"If you'd been here," she went on, her voice rising despite herself, "he wouldn't have died."

Thall stepped forward.

Sakura lifted her hand, stopping him without a word. She faced Lea.

"I'm sorry I couldn't be there," Sakura said, holding her gaze.

The apology broke something.

"That's not enough," Lea said, restraint finally giving way. "You're supposed to be there. That's what you do. You fix things."

Her voice wavered, then sharpened. "It isn't fair."

Ashe pressed close, whining low.

Silence fell, heavy and close.

"I lost my best friend," Thall said, breaking it. His voice stayed level, without distance. "Recently. I'm not past it yet."

Lea's shoulders tightened, but she did not turn.

"But I won't let it stop me," he continued. "I know what he'd want. He'd want me standing. Moving. Living."

He paused. "I think your friend would want the same."

Lea's breath caught. The anger turned in on itself, leaving her without support. She dropped to her knees, grief breaking through in raw sobs she no longer restrained. Ashe sat beside her, whining softly and nudging her with his nose.

Sakura turned toward the stairs.

"I'm going to make tea," she said gently. "It would help, it's good for you."

Lea forced herself upright, wiping her face with her sleeve. She shook her head.

"No," she said hoarsely.

She turned and left.

Outside, Scarlet waited, still and patient. Ashe stayed close at Lea's side.

Thall crossed to the door and closed it behind them.

The practice fell quiet.

Chapter 22: Sight Of The Sun

Morning arrived without urgency. Thall was not needed in the practice, and Sakura did not ask him to remain. With his sword at his side and his shield across his back, he went to the board near the temple, taking small jobs between short escorts and bits of labor within the village.

Sakura opened the practice on her own. The pace eased from the day before. No injuries came through from Harlan's side, and what remained was work she could manage without strain. A few new cases arrived at uneven intervals, nothing that pressed the room into haste.

Night came to the Hollow.

Thall returned as Sakura was cleaning for the day, water darkened from use, cloth laid out to dry. He took a broom without comment and worked beside her, the space returning to order with quiet efficiency.

When they finished, he rested the broom against the wall. "I was thinking of heading to the temple," he said.

Sakura glanced toward the door. "I'd like to come with you."

Thall considered it, then nodded. "All right."

She banked the lamps, leaving only enough light to move safely. Outside, the yards were still active, but the noise no longer pressed against the walls. Night lay across the Hollow.

Sakura followed a step behind him as they headed toward the temple, noting the certainty in his stride as the distance closed.

Lea was already there.

She stood near the alcove to the side where the candles were kept. Her hands rested at her sides, still, her attention turned inward rather than toward the room.

Sakura saw her at once. She crossed the space without hurry and took her place beside her. No words passed between them. They stood together, heads bowed, allowing the quiet to do what neither tried to guide.

Thall entered and stopped a short distance back. He understood the space for what it was, meant for presence rather than speech. He waited, giving them room.

After a time, the three of them raised their heads toward the alcove, the small flames casting steady light across the stone.

Lea took a candle and lit it from the shared flame. She kept it steady, eyes on the wick as it caught.

"For Thorne," she said quietly.

She set it in its place and stepped back.

Thall followed without pause. He took another candle and lit it, his hand steady.

"For Eldrin," he said.

Sakura watched them both, then reached for a third. She paused only long enough to confirm her intent.

"For those who never made it far enough to be named," she said, and placed it beside the others.

They stood together in silence, the candles burning evenly between them.

When they left the temple, the Hollow lay under night. The yards were quieter, reduced to distant movement and the occasional call. Outside the steps, Ashe waited where she had been left, rising as Lea approached. Scarlet stood nearby, wings folded, head lowered as Lea rested a hand briefly against her neck.

"If you are free in the morning," Sakura said lightly, "you are welcome to come by. I can make tea."

Lea hesitated for only a moment. A familiar bird perched on a nearby post lifted and flew toward a figure at the edge of her sight. She could not be certain it was meant for her.

She then nodded. "I would like that."

She turned toward the path leading away from the temple, leading scarlet, and Ashe falling into step beside her.

Thall and Sakura went the other way, the practice already dark when they returned.

Thall set his shield down and drew his sword. He laid a cloth across the table before taking up the whetstone.

The sound stayed low and even. He worked the edge with careful attention, not to sharpen so much as to confirm it. When he finished, he wiped the blade clean, oiled it lightly, and set it back within reach.

Sakura banked the last lamp and went upstairs without speaking.

That night, sleep came more easily.

◆ ◆ ◆

Early the next morning, Sakura had the water heating by the time Lea arrived, Thall already awake and seated near the table. Ashe waited near the door while Scarlet remained outside, calm and watchful.

The tea was herbal and simple, fragrant without being sweet, chosen for steadiness rather than flavor. They drank it slowly, sharing a small bite of bread. At first, little was said.

"You do this every morning?" Lea asked at last.

Sakura nodded. "When I can."

Lea adjusted slightly. She took another sip before setting the cup down. "It helps," she said.

The quiet returned, unforced.

"I did not have a surname before," Lea said. "I use one now."

Thall looked at her, attentive.

"Bramble," she continued. "It was his clan name."

Thall remained still.

"Thorne," Lea added. "I took it because I wanted him to keep walking beside me." Her fingers tightened briefly around the cup. "I did not want his name to feel like loss. I wanted it to be something I could stand inside."

Thall nodded once. "Eldrin would poke fun at that," he said quietly.

Lea glanced at him and smiled.

"He was my closest friend," Thall went on. "I was not steady enough when it mattered."

Sakura allowed the silence to remain a moment, then set another cup on the table and poured.

Lea released a breath, quiet but real.

When they finished, Sakura stayed behind as the day began to stir, returning to the practice.

Thall and Lea stepped outside together, Ashe rising at once to join them. Scarlet remained near the practice door, calm and watchful, her gaze tracking Thall as he passed, attentive in a way it had not been moments before.

At the board, they paused and read in silence.

When Lea indicated a posting, she said quietly, "I used to do this with Thorne."

Thall reached up and marked it without hesitation.

The work itself was unremarkable, a delivery that required timing along a route skirting unstable ground. Lea moved with the ease of someone who read the land by habit, adjusting their path without breaking pace. She indicated where the land would give, where wind cut sharper than it looked, where the straight line was the wrong choice.

Thall followed her lead, attentive but slower to take it in. His instincts favored close threat and clear distance, the certainty of a blade over the quieter reading of ground and movement.

Still, he adapted. He asked when he needed to and watched when he did not.

They completed the job without incident and reported back as required. Ashe stayed at Lea's side while the clerk marked the delivery and counted payment. Scarlet waited outside the office, still and patient, her presence noted without comment.

After that, they returned to the practice. Lea lingered while Sakura cleaned her tools, watching in silence until Sakura spoke without lifting her eyes.

"I don't know how to let go of what I've lost," Lea said.

Sakura finished her task and set the cloth aside before answering.

"You don't," she said. "You learn where to carry it."

Lea nodded once, as if the words confirmed something already forming.

She straightened. "I should go."

"Where are you staying?" Sakura asked, calm and even.

Lea paused, then let out a breath. "At the inn."

Sakura considered her; careful not to press. "I have rooms upstairs," she said. "Three of them are empty. You could take one, if you want."

Lea hesitated.

"There's no cost," Sakura added. "And no obligation." Her gaze flicked toward the stairs. "Company can be its own kind of healing."

"And Scarlet?" Lea asked.

"There is a beast house attached," Sakura said. "It hasn't been used in some time, but it is sound."

Lea considered, then nodded once.

"I can help at the practice," she said. "Not the way you do, and not like a keeper. I know splints and wraps. I know how to hold someone steady until you get there."

Sakura nodded. "You are a tamer. I do not expect you to be anything else."

Lea did not answer at once. "I never said I was one," she replied.

Sakura paused. Her gaze moved from Lea to Scarlet, then to Ashe. She took them in before speaking.

"You travel with a skymare," she said. "And a hound."

"Ashe was bound to Thorne," Lea said. "Not to me." She hesitated, then added, "Scarlet is not bound at all."

Sakura listened without interrupting.

"Everyone else thinks the same," Lea said quietly. "And I never correct them."

Her gaze moved from Sakura to Thall and back again, quick and searching.

Sakura inclined her head once.

Thall spoke then, voice even. "That is not for me to tell."

Lea drew a breath through her teeth.

"I need to close out my room," she said. "And bring my things."

Thall straightened from across the room, setting the whetstone aside. "I can help."

Lea glanced at him, then nodded. "Thank you."

They left together. Ashe fell in beside them. Scarlet waited, then pressed close to Thall, brushing against him with easy familiarity.

Lea noticed, smiled, and said nothing.

Sakura returned to the counter and began putting her tools away.

That was the first night they closed the practice together.

Chapter 23: Five Years OF Dust

During the next five years, the practice learned to remain open.

At first, it stayed open because it had to. Injuries did not wait for bells, and hunters were often brought in late, blood already darkened, pain already rooted. Beasts calmed only after nightfall, when handlers had lost daylight and restraint together. Lamps burned long past dusk. Shelves were tended with care born of exhaustion rather than preference.

What began as necessity became routine. The door stopped closing early. Dusk passed without comment. Locking it at all grew rare, then fell away.

The Hollow changed with it. Wounds reached clean hands sooner. Infections took fewer lives. Mornings saw fewer stretchers carried out beneath the fog.

When Sakura's required term ended and her standing was confirmed, the work no longer waited on temple approval. Along with Thall, and Lea, they had saved enough coin to take possession of the building together.

One of the rooms on the second floor filled over time, shelves crowded with herbs, powders, and oils lining the walls. Vessels simmered through the night. Salves, tonics, and restoratives took shape there, alongside the quiet study of books gathered over years rather than assigned. Sakura resumed her work in alchemy.

Dustin and Sybil came into her care not long after, two young summoners, disciplined and attentive, their aptitude lying in careful arcane manipulation rather than instinct or bond. Sakura trained them as a keeper would, hands meant to be steady, to assess and carry care forward without her presence beside them. What Harlan once bore alone spread naturally among them. They learned to clean wounds, brace breaks, regulate pain through precise arcane application, and recognize danger before it bloomed.

Work reached into the dark hours. Nights grew busy. Dawn grew quiet.

With capable hands beneath the roof, Sakura no longer needed to remain every hour. Some days stretched farther beyond the walls. Some mornings she rode out beside Thall or walked with Lea toward work that carried them past the Hollow's edge. She left without worry, knowing what waited behind her would endure.

When she returned, lamps still burned.

Life in the Hollow always shaped those who stayed.

Thall stopped moving like a man passing through. He trained alongside the hunters of the Hollow, tamers and summoners alike, until their rhythms became his own. His sword work sharpened through repetition rather than instruction, footwork formed by uneven ground and narrow passes instead of drills. The shield became natural in his grip, steady and sure, no longer something he compensated for, only something he carried with confidence.

He began to read the land the way those in the Hollow did. He walked routes before dawn, traced ridgelines, learned how wind bent through cuts in the rock and how sound carried across open ground. Paths revealed themselves through use rather than map or lecture. On longer routes, Lea allowed him to take Scarlet with him, the skymare moving at his side with ease that made the miles pass differently. She carried no burden, but her presence changed the work, and Thall adjusted quickly.

In time, Roland used him more often, placing him where decisions needed to be made without delay. Thall answered without comment, and soon others looked to him for guidance. Scarlet came with him on those journeys as well.

Among tamers and summoners, his presence stopped being remarked upon, not because it faded, but because it endured. He became someone others adjusted around without thought, dependable in the way of stone set where it mattered.

When whispers of Dominion doctrine began to surface beyond Eldhar and drift into Aetherwind through trade routes and temple correspondence, Thall recognized them for what they were. The language carried a familiar edge. It drew his attention tighter rather than dulling it, memory filling the gaps where explanation no longer belonged.

Lea became a familiar presence in the Hollow. The assumption that she was a tamer took root early and was never corrected. She spoke little of herself, and no one pressed. Olivia and Ethan came under her care in time, both tamers, both young, and she guided them with the same patience she brought to everything else. Awareness came first. Control followed only when it was earned.

Master Roland trusted her judgment in the yards and beyond them. He began assigning her work without supervision, then without accompaniment. Reports returned clean and tasks concluded without note. When difficulty rose, Lea was the one sent to meet it, most often alone, Ashe at her side, the hound learning her pace and intent until they moved as one without signal.

Somewhere along the way, the bow was set aside. Lea took to steel instead, a dagger in each hand, their use shaped through repetition and restraint. Distance stopped being a barrier once the rope dart joined her kit, its weight familiar at her side, always ready. She learned how to enter and leave without being marked, how to let shadow and terrain swallow sound, how to be present only when she chose.

In time, her name began to carry quietly. Lea Bramble, spoken without emphasis and understood without explanation. Among tamers and summoners alike, it became accepted that when she was sent, the work would be done.

Her summoning remained unspoken. Beyond the Hollow, away from paths and watchers, she continued her training alone. Each attempt was careful. Each success contained. What answered her did so rarely, and she guarded the knowledge with greater discipline than the act itself required.

As survivability in Guardian's Hollow improved, morale followed, and trade increased until coin moved more freely through hands that trusted the work being done. The yards ran smoother as well, and the Hollow moved beyond mere endurance into something capable of adapting.

That was when the doctrine began to feel closer, not arriving loudly or announcing itself, but threading into language and expectation, into the quiet understanding of which questions no longer received answers. The Hollow noticed, even as it resisted.

◆ ◆ ◆

One evening, that resistance was tested.

The tavern was loud in the way the Hollow preferred, noise shaped by familiarity rather than chaos. Thall sat at one of the long tables with Sakura and Lea, a meal half-finished between them. He had loosened his grip on the day but had not yet let it go.

Two hunters stood near the bar, close enough that their words carried without effort.

"They don't just conquer," the first said, tipping his mug back before setting it down again. "The Dominion finds a place for everything. It puts order where there was none, and you can't deny that."

The other hunter snorted and leaned an elbow on the bar. "That's not order. That's control dressed up to look clean."

"Maybe," the first replied, unbothered. "But it works. Look at Eldhar. Look how long it lasted."

"They lasted because people were afraid," the second said, shaking his head. "Fear isn't strength. It only lasts until it doesn't."

The first shrugged. "Fear keeps people in line. Aetherwind could use a little of that. Too much freedom makes people careless."

"Careless?" Thall said.

The word carried farther than it should have, and the tavern changed around it. He was on his feet before the scrape of his chair finished registering.

Both hunters turned.

"You don't know what you're talking about," Thall said, stepping closer. His hand was not on his sword, but his posture carried the same certainty. "You think the Dominion finds a place for people. What it does is decide what they're allowed to be."

The first hunter frowned. "I wasn't—"

"You just haven't lived long enough under it to recognize the shape," Thall said.

The second hunter shifted uneasily, glancing between them. "Thall, it's just talk."

"It stops being talk when people start repeating it," Thall replied, his voice steady, edged. "That's how it begins, with someone saying it works and someone else deciding it belongs, until one day you realize the questions you used to ask no longer receive answers."

The first hunter opened his mouth, then closed it.

Sakura was already standing. She did not touch Thall. She stepped into his line of sight, calm and steady, grounding the moment without challenging it.

"That's enough," she said quietly.

Lea moved to his other side and allowed her presence to register, close enough to be known without drawing his eyes. "Not here," she added, her voice low. "Not like this."

Thall stayed where he was for another breath, eyes locked on the man at the bar. The tavern had gone quieter than before, attention drawn in despite no one choosing to look.

Then he let the breath go.

He stepped back hard, boots scraping wood as he broke the line he had cut through the room. Chairs scraped. Someone muttered under their breath.

"Believe what you want," he said, his voice carrying past the hunters and into the room at large. "Just don't pretend it's harmless."

He turned and drove for the door, shoulder clipping the frame as he shoved it open. Cold air rushed in after him, and the door slammed hard enough to rattle the hinges.

Cold air hit his face as he stepped outside, sharp and bracing. He did not slow. His boots carried him away from the light, away from the noise, anger still burning hot enough that he could not yet turn it into anything useful.

Behind him, the tavern found its noise again, though it returned unevenly and without its earlier ease.

Sakura and Lea exchanged a glance before following, neither of them surprised that this time, he did not choose silence.

Chapter 24: A True Bond

Thall returned late one afternoon, dust still clinging to his boots from the road. Scarlet walked at his shoulder without lead or pressure, wings folded tight as he guided her toward the beast house attached to the practice. The structure had taken on a new purpose over time, its stalls widened and reinforced to suit her frame. He secured her there with care, checking straps and space before leaving her.

He entered through the back door connecting the stables to the practice, expecting sound. Instead, the space lay quiet.

Dustin and Sybil were gone. The racks stood orderly. Only Sakura remained, seated near the far table, hands occupied with her notes.

"Where is everyone?" Thall asked.

Sakura looked up. "I sent my trainees on an errand," she said. "They will return before evening."

A voice answered from the shadow near the wall. "I finished my work early."

Thall turned. Lea stood where the light fell uneven, arms loose at her sides. He had not noticed her presence, and the realization caught him off guard.

He cleared his throat. "Scarlet's in the stable," he said. "She did well on the road."

"I'm sure of it," Lea replied.

She stepped forward slightly. "There's something we need to discuss."

Thall tipped his head, waiting.

Lea drew a breath. "I want you to have Scarlet. Properly."

He frowned. "That isn't necessary."

"She chooses you," Lea said. "Every time."

Sakura closed her book. "Lea spoke to me about it earlier," she said. "I agree."

Thall looked between them. "She isn't something to be passed along."

"She isn't being passed," Lea replied. "She's being placed where she already belongs."

He hesitated, then shook his head once. "That's not something I can take lightly."

"You don't have to," Lea said. "It's already decided."

Silence followed.

Then Thall stepped forward and drew her into a brief embrace, unguarded and genuine. "Thank you," he said.

214

He left soon after, coin already in hand, plan in mind.

By the time he returned, dusk had claimed the yard. Scarlet now wore new barding fitted to her frame, plates worked to mirror the pattern of his new chain mail while leaving her wings free. She bore it easily, pride evident in her posture.

Later, they gathered around the kitchen table on the second floor. Sakura poured tea. Lea sat with her hands folded, watching.

Thall entered last and set two bundles on the table.

"Scarlet and I are not the only ones with new gear," he said. "It's time we all looked like what we've become."

He slid the first bundle toward Sakura. White robes from Hanzhong lay folded within, healer runes worked along the edges in green that matched the Lianhua Dynasty's colors. Beside them rested a staff, simple and balanced, an orb set at its crown. A mender's staff.

Sakura's hands went still.

The second bundle went to Lea. Leather gear reinforced at the shoulders with arcane crystal, suited to summoners and tamers alike. A purple cloak followed, its silver lining catching the light in a pattern echoing Aetherwind's colors.

"These are gifts," Thall said. "Not payment. Appreciation."

Neither woman spoke at first. Then Sakura inclined her head and thanked him, her voice warm and sincere. Lea followed with a quiet word of thanks.

Soon after, they gathered the bundles and stepped away, already testing fit and weight, the room easing as the gifts found their places.

Lea stepped out first.

The leather fit her cleanly, the arcane crystal at the shoulders catching the light without drawing it. The cloak rested along her frame with ease, the silver lining tracing her movement rather than announcing it.

Thall looked up and smiled. "You wear it well."

Lea lifted a brow, pleased. "It feels right."

A moment later, Sakura emerged.

The white robes sat precisely, the green runes along the edges subtle and exact. The staff rested easily in her hand, the orb at its crown reflecting the lamplight in soft halos. She appeared composed, assured, and quietly striking.

Thall stopped short. His mouth stayed open longer than he intended.

Lea reached out and tapped his chin upward. "You can breathe," she said lightly.

Sakura's lips curved, faint but genuine.

Thall cleared his throat, color rising in his face. "You look... remarkable," he managed.

The night passed without disturbance, yet something took shape among them, quiet and unforced. Trust deepened through shared ease rather than words.

◆ ◆ ◆

The common area grew busy in the way it often did after midmorning. People crossed it with purpose, lingering only when necessary. A few stalls had been set along the inner edge of the yard, and a line had formed near a table where notices were sometimes posted.

Thall and Lea moved through the common yard without hurry. Sakura walked with them. She had stepped away from the practice without concern, leaving it in the care of Dustin and Sybil.

They were nearly across the yard when the horn sounded.

It cut hard and deliberate through the air. Conversation ceased as if drawn tight. Beasts behind iron shifted, then calmed again beneath practiced hands. Movement continued but narrowed into lines. People turned without instruction, eyes drawn toward the inner gate.

Lea stopped beside Thall, Sakura close at her other side. Ashe's head lifted, ears forward, body still. Scarlet waited a few paces behind them, wings folded close, her stance calm but ready.

Thall kept his eyes on the gate.

A messenger entered first, riding at a controlled pace atop a skymare, as if even the beast had been trained not to startle the yard. A cloth draped across the skymare's chest and flanks bore Aetherwind's colors, deep purple edged in silver, secured to allow full use of her wings. Her coat was white and unmarred, her mane a muted gold. The wings rested tight at her sides, a faint gold fading to white where they met the body. She moved with quiet authority, drawing attention without noise.

The man wore a clean cloak pinned with the crest of Aetherwind, a silver-worked circle against deep purple. Arcane symbols traced the edge in precise order, each mark deliberate and evenly spaced.

Six soldiers followed, armored and spaced with intent, each alert in a way that suggested readiness rather than ceremony. Their plates were clean but unpolished, the same crest etched rather than raised, silver lines catching the light only as they moved.

The messenger dismounted with ease. One of the soldiers passed him a scroll from its case and stepped back into formation.

Chapter 25: The Steward's Seal

Roland was already there, standing near the gate as if he had been waiting long before the horn sounded. He watched the messenger and the escort the way he watched a new beast brought into the yards.

The messenger raised his voice, so it carried without strain. "By order of the Crown of Aetherwind," he said. "This notice applies to every village and holding under Aetherwind protection."

The crowd stayed still. A few leaned forward without realizing it, as though the meaning might pass them by if they did not.

The messenger continued. "The Crown remains committed to protecting the Arcane way of life. We will not permit foreign doctrine to reshape our people through quiet pressure or negotiation."

Thall felt a slight lift in his chest, not relief but recognition. It was the sense of someone choosing a direction at last, rather than pretending neutrality could survive on its own.

The messenger opened the scroll fully and continued without pause. "Effective immediately, any business conducted with the Dominion will incur a new tax. A Steward will be assigned to each village and major holding. That Steward will collect and oversee all transactions involving the Dominion in any form."

A murmur passed through the yard, low and uneven. It was not outrage. It was the beginning of argument that had not yet found language.

The messenger did not allow space for response. "This is not punishment," he said. "It is protection. Trade that strengthens the Dominion increases pressure against our people. If you deal with them, you will do so openly, and you will bear the cost."

A man near the front spoke. "We trade because we need to. You think the Crown will replace what they supply?"

The messenger cleared his throat and adjusted his grip on the scroll. He lifted it slightly, eyes returning to the parchment.

"By order of the Crown," he read, voice steady, "all taxes levied on trade conducted with the Lianhua Dynasty are reduced by half, effective immediately."

Sound rippled through the yard before anyone stopped it.

The messenger raised his gaze. "The Crown will reinforce supply lines where reinforcement is possible," he said. "But you will not feed the Dominion and claim necessity. The law will no longer treat ignorance as virtue."

"This could hurt us," someone called.

Others nodded. A few shook their heads. Some did not react at all, faces blank in the way people learned when they did not wish to stand clearly on either side.

Thall looked toward Roland.

Roland's expression remained unchanged. He did not look impressed. He looked like a man watching flame build too close to dry timber.

The messenger read the final lines. "Stewards will arrive within the month. Resistance to Steward authority will be treated as disruption of Crown order. The Crown requests your cooperation and your patience. This measure is intended to protect our future."

The soldiers did not move until he did. They mounted and departed in the same controlled order, leaving the yard to absorb what had been placed into it.

◆ ◆ ◆

As the gate closed, sound returned in pieces. It did not resume as before. It fractured into smaller groups and tighter voices.

Lea watched the crowd a moment, then looked at Thall. "At least they're trying," she said.

"They are," he replied. "They're applying pressure where it matters."

She tilted her head. "And the Hollow will stir."

Thall nodded. "Because it will turn people against each other here, not against the Dominion."

Lea's mouth drew thin. "Anger here doesn't stay quiet."

They began walking again, avoiding the densest clusters, listening without intending to.

A tamer near the wall said, "So now the Crown taxes us for surviving."

Another answered, "They're taxing Dominion influence."

"That's easy to say when you aren't feeding a family," the first replied.

Thall kept his eyes forward. He had learned early that people spoke most honestly when they believed no one of consequence was listening.

A rasping voice behind them said, "Stewards will become watchers. You'll see. They'll call it protection and start counting us like the Dominion does."

Another voice replied, "Or maybe we've been too comfortable pretending trade carries no cost."

Lea's hands stayed at her sides. Ashe remained close.

Sakura adjusted the bundle in her arms. "People will blame the wrong target."

"They might," Thall said. "It's still a line drawn."

Sakura's eyes drifted back toward the gate. "A line invites response."

Lea nodded once. "And Stewards invite resentment."

Sakura looked at her. "This will draw attention beyond trade."

Lea did not deny it. "I know."

Sakura's voice lowered. "The practice will function. The trainees can manage the work. If unrest grows, skill alone won't keep them safe."

They separated without further discussion. Lea patted Scarlet before turning away, Ashe already at her side as she headed back toward the yards. Sakura moved toward the practice, her pace unhurried but directed.

Thall watched Sakura go, his gaze lingering just long enough for a faint smile to break through. "A beauty," he murmured, then turned, mounted Scarlet, and rode out to complete a job he had accepted earlier.

◆ ◆ ◆

By nightfall, the Hollow had gone quiet. It was not calm. It was contained.

Thall climbed the stairs to his room and closed the door. The space was small, familiar, and plain. He placed his gear where it belonged and sat without lighting the lamp.

The horn still rang in his thoughts, carrying with it the sense of a kingdom pressing back, of a system tightening, of people being pushed toward choices they had avoided.

He stood and sorted through a shelf where he kept things he rarely touched: old cord, a cracked tin cup, a folded bundle of cloth he never used but never discarded.

His hand brushed something heavier.

His old travel bag sat half-collapsed in the corner, worn by years and ignored longer still. He had not used it since the early days, when distance felt like an enemy rather than a tool.

He did not know why he reached for it. He drew it out and set it on the bed, intending to clear it away, a task he had delayed more than once. When he opened it, the flap protested softly, dust and the scent of old road rising with it.

He reached inside without looking.

Paper brushed his fingers.

He froze, heat rising in his face.

He drew it out slowly. A sealed letter, dry and intact, the seal almost broken, its edges worn from being carried too long. His thumb traced the seal as recognition took shape. He did not need light to know it.

Once, he had carried it with purpose, when he still believed intention could shield people from what followed.

His breath caught, then steadied, his grip tightening until the paper bent.

He had left home with this letter in his pack more than five years earlier, telling himself the road mattered, that he would return, that necessity excused delay.

He stared at it until his eyes burned, he then lit the lamp. The seal marked it as a temple message, addressed to the temple of Hanzhong.

Memory surfaced. The way it had been placed in his hands. The way no one had told him its contents. The way he had accepted it anyway, because refusal demanded questions, and questions were dangerous in Serenthall.

He sat on the edge of the bed with the letter in both hands.

What rose in him was neither clean grief nor clean anger. It was the awareness that the letter had continued while he had not, that time had moved elsewhere without regard for him. Eldrin's face returned as it had on the last night they spoke. The merchant's voice followed, calm and transactional.

Then his family came, unbidden.

His mother's hands, always moving. Garrick's voice, firm even when gentle. Celestia as she had been when he left, still young enough to believe absence could be temporary. Five years without a word. Five years without sending anything back.

He had avoided those thoughts not out of care, but because opening them demanded more than he had offered.

His eyes dropped to the seal.

A tear escaped, cutting a clear line down his cheek before he noticed it. He did not wipe it away. He stood there, thumb resting near the wax, and let the moment move through him without resistance.

If he had delivered it that day, he would have been at the temple instead of the market. He would not have collapsed. He might have returned sooner; or at least tried. In that difference alone, he would have been there.

His fingers moved to the edge of the seal.

He could break it and read what had been important enough to pull him from home on the day his friend died.

He stayed still, breath controlled, shoulders squared as if posture could resist consequence. After a moment, he lowered his hands slightly and looked at the wax.

He did not break the seal. He did not set the letter aside.

The silence that followed felt less like rest than waiting.

Chapter 26: The Letter That Waited

Thall did not sit back down.

The letter stayed in his hand, unopened, the wax dull in the lamplight. He remained standing another moment, as if listening for something that no longer answered, then turned.

He crossed the narrow hall and knocked once on Sakura's door.

It opened after the second knock. She had not undressed fully, a habit she had never quite lost. Her gaze went first to the sealed letter.

"What's wrong?" she asked, her voice low.

"I need you," he said.

She stepped back without question.

He moved on down the hall and knocked on Lea's door.

She answered almost at once, already awake, hair loose, expression alert without surprise as she opened it partway.

"I can't do this alone," he said quietly.

She saw his face, then nodded once. He turned before she could answer.

They gathered in the small kitchen off the hall, sleep still clinging to them, the table worn smooth by years of gentle use. Thall placed the letter between them, his fingers resting near the seal.

"I was sent with it," he said, voice even. "They told me it was routine delivery. I reached Hanzhong before dusk."

His fingers brushed the edge of the seal, then pulled back.

"They turned me away at the hall," he continued. "I arrived too late in the day."

"The next morning, I was too early, so they told me to return at first bell. I went into the market." His jaw tightened once. "That's where I heard the news, the execution"

His hand closed tight. Neither of his friends spoke, the last trace of sleep gone from them.

"By the time I came to, first bell had already passed." His gaze stayed on the table. "I didn't stay. I didn't go home. I spent my days where noise kept thought away. When work came that carried me from Eldhar, I took it."

Sakura nodded slowly. "I remember," she said.

"I didn't mean to forget it." His palm rested flat near the seal. "I didn't wake you because I know what this says. I woke you because I don't."

No one moved. The lamplight flickered once.

Then he broke the seal.

The sound was soft, barely there, yet it struck harder than the horn earlier that day. He unfolded the paper with care and read.

His breath slipped out thin. Whatever he saw did not ask for words, and he gave none. Sakura watched the color drain from his face. She reached out without asking.

She read aloud. The opening was formal, filled with acknowledgment, gratitude, and statements of cooperation between patrols. Her voice remained level until it could not.

"...we thank the Hanzhong patrol for their diligence in detaining Eldrin of Stonefield, found attempting to cross into Hanzhong territory without proper documentation..."

Lea's hand tightened against the table.

"...in accordance with standing agreements, the individual was transferred to Dominion authorities for resolution."

Sakura swallowed and continued.

"...the matter will be addressed. This notice confirms the action taken on the date of transfer."

She stopped.

Thall stared at the table, the grain of the wood sharp in his vision. Henry's face surfaced without warning, calm and careful as it had always been. The memory did not rage. It lay there, unmoving.

"They sent me away," he said quietly. "That day."

Neither interrupted.

"Henry knew," Thall went on. "Or suspected. Enough to move me. Enough to keep me from being there."

The knowledge did not break him the way Eldrin's death had. It pressed inward instead, dense and exacting. He rose, the chair scraping once against stone.

"I won't stand idle," he said, certainty steadying his voice.

"I don't know what this will bring. I don't know how far it reaches." He looked from Lea to Sakura. "I would want your help. But I won't ask it as debt. If you walk away, I will understand."

Sakura folded the letter carefully and set it back on the table. "I'm not leaving," she said.

Lea nodded once. "Neither am I."

They remained there, the letter between them, the lamp burning low. For a time, no one spoke.

At last, Sakura rose. She moved behind Thall and rested her hand on his shoulder, the touch light but sure. He reached back and closed his fingers around hers, grounding himself in contact before releasing it.

"You'll need rest," she said quietly.

He nodded once.

She crossed the hall with purpose, to the back room where her medicines waited, jars and vials aligned in careful order. When she returned, she placed a small vial in his hand.

"This will help you sleep," she said. "It won't dull you. It will give you quiet."

He drank without comment and went to his room. Sleep did not come at once, but when it did, it took him fully.

Sakura and Lea stayed at the table after he left.

"We need to watch him," Lea said at last. "Make sure he doesn't turn sharp in the wrong places."

Sakura inclined her head. "I know."

They dimmed the lamp and returned to their rooms.

◆ ◆ ◆

Thall woke later than usual, light already higher than expected when his eyes opened. He lay still a moment, listening to the building, the Hollow awake without him. He dressed quickly, routine steadying his thoughts, then went down the hall toward the kitchen.

Lea sat at the table with a book open before her, though her attention was elsewhere. Ashe lay at her feet, head resting against her boot, watchful even at ease. Lea's brow was drawn, focus turned inward.

"Morning," Thall said.

She looked up, surprise flickering before it faded. "Morning."

He took the chair across from her, studying her briefly. "You look like you didn't sleep."

She shook her head slightly. "I did. Just thinking."

"About what?"

She hesitated, then shrugged once. "A job. Or whether to take it."

Before he could ask more, the kettle gave a sharp whistle from the hearth. Lea rose at once, moved to it on instinct, and poured the water with care. They drank in silence, steam lifting between them, warmth easing some of the edge from the room.

After a while, Lea spoke again. "I stopped at Arcane Peak recently. A job took me near it."

Thall glanced up. "You didn't mention it."

"I didn't think it mattered." She reached into her side pouch and drew out a narrow silver tally, engraved clean and precise. "I brought my birth parchment. They verified it and issued my identification."

Thall blinked, then smiled. "That's no small thing. Congratulations."

She inclined her head and returned the tally to her side, her fingers lingering a heartbeat longer than needed.

When Thall finished his tea, he set the cup aside and leaned forward slightly, lowering his voice. "I'm planning something this evening. I'd like you back earlier than usual, if you can manage it."

She studied him, then nodded. "I'll try." She lifted her book again, burying herself in it with intent.

Thall went downstairs.

Sybil was already in motion, spinning a pair of forceps until Dustin snapped at her to stop. She grinned and slipped away just out of reach.

"You can't treat the practice like a playground," Dustin said sharply.

"I'm not," Sybil replied. "Playgrounds are cleaner."

Thall cleared his throat. "Where's Sakura?"

"Herb room," Dustin said. "She's been there most of the morning."

Thall nodded. "I've got something planned tonight. Stay close."

Sybil's eyes brightened. Dustin frowned but said nothing.

Thall moved through the market stalls with purpose, his steps quick and sure, as though the path had already been chosen. When he returned hours later, energy carried in his stride that hadn't been there before.

He paused at the archery range. Ethan and Olivia practiced, arrows thudding into scarred targets.

"Tonight," Thall said. "If you're free."

They exchanged looks, then nodded.

Back at the practice, Sakura remained among her herbs, Sybil tending a patient, Dustin assisting another. Thall went upstairs and sat on the edge of his bed, hands resting on his knees. His heart beat hard enough that he felt it in his throat.

When he looked up again, the light outside had dimmed. Evening was closing in.

He rose, adjusted his gear in the mirror, took a steadying breath, and went back downstairs.

Sakura stood near the central table. Dustin, Sybil, Olivia, and Ethan were nearby. Ashe lay curled in the corner, eyes half closed.

Sakura looked at him. "Did you call us together?"

He nodded. "Is Lea back?"

Ethan shook his head. "She stepped out a while ago."

Time stretched. Darkness deepened beyond the windows.

Thall's shoulders lowered, disappointment flickering before he hid it.

"She might be late," Sakura said gently. "If the job ran long."

Thall hesitated. Then he looked at Sakura, resolve passing through him, and crossed the room toward her with intent.

Chapter 27: Witnesses

Thall had asked a few people to remain at the practice.

Sybil lingered near the benches, unable to stay still. Ethan and Olivia stood close together, their low conversation trailing off whenever it threatened to become more than murmured speculation. Dustin remained a little apart, posture straight, hands placed behind his back as if waiting for instruction.

Ashe lay in the corner, her head down, eyes half-lidded but alert.

Lea had not arrived.

The light outside thinned, evening pressing closer, and Thall felt the weight of time sliding past what he had planned. He drew a steady breath and stepped toward the center of the room.

"Sakura," he said, extending her his hand.

Her attention fixed on him at once. She crossed the space with slow, deliberate steps, awareness sharpening in her eyes as she stopped in front of him.

He took both of her hands, turning fully toward her. His gaze found hers and stayed there.

Sybil made a small, breathless sound and clapped a hand over her mouth.

Color rose in Sakura's cheeks. "Thall," she began, then stopped, surprise catching as she searched his face.

He glanced toward the others, drawing them in without words. "I wanted everyone here," he said, voice even, "because I don't want to hide this."

Sakura drew her right hand back and pressed it to her chest, breath caught somewhere between disbelief and feeling. Quiet excitement rippled through the room. Sybil bounced on her heels. Ethan and Dustin stared as if afraid to blink. Olivia flushed deep red, eyes wide, hands clasped tight in front of her.

Sakura stood without words.

Thall freed one hand and reached into the pouch at his side. He drew out a ring, a green stone set in mithril, simple and clean. He took her left hand with care and slid the ring onto her finger.

"You've been beside me," he said. "From the beginning. You never turned away. You never asked me to be anything other than what I was becoming. You stayed when I doubted myself, and you were steady when I could not be."

Sakura's eyes shone as the ring came to rest on her finger.

That was when Sybil lost what restraint she had left. "Kiss her!"

Ethan froze. Dustin looked like he had forgotten how to breathe. Olivia turned away and then back again, mortified and unable to look elsewhere.

Thall leaned in. Sakura met him halfway. The kiss was unhurried, gentle, and certain.

Applause broke out just as a familiar voice sounded from the doorway, warm and unmistakable.

"It's about time," Lea said.

She stood there with a faint smile, Ashe coming to her side.

The room erupted.

Laughter rose. Hands clapped shoulders and backs. Someone poured drinks. Someone else pulled chairs into a loose circle. The night carried on in shared warmth, voices light, the kind of joy that did not need explanation to last.

Eventually, one by one, they turned in.

But the feeling remained.

◆ ◆ ◆

Thall woke next morning, with pale light already through the high windows, thin against the stone.

He dressed without hurry. The shield went across his back, familiar weight finding its place. The sword followed at his side.

Down the hall, the kitchen was awake before the rest of the floor. Breakfast had been laid out with care. Warm bread. Fruit cut clean. Tea already poured. A folded note rested against the cup.

Eat. You forget when you're thinking too much. I'll see you downstairs.

He smiled despite himself and ate slower than usual. When he finished, he rinsed the cup and set it back where it had been.

Voices carried from below. Sakura's, calm and even. Another answering her, older. Paper moved. The faint scrape of a chair.

He took the stairs two at a time and entered the lower hall.

Sakura stood near one of the long tables, sleeves drawn back, hands busy beside Sybil. Across from them, Dustin worked through a stack of records, eyes down, lips moving as he counted under his breath.

"Morning," Thall said.

"Morning." The answer came from all of them. Sakura's voice was there with the rest, softer than usual. Color rose to her cheeks before she looked away.

She crossed the space as he reached the last step and rose onto her toes, a brief kiss pressed to his lips. He leaned into it.

"Thank you for the food," he said quietly.

She smiled, small and pleased, then turned back to the table.

The knock came then another, firm and deliberate.

Dustin looked up first. Sybil stilled. Sakura turned toward the door as Thall moved ahead of her.

High Priest Liang stood on the threshold. High Priest Aika waited just behind him.

Everyone bowed at once.

Liang inclined his head in return. Aika's gaze moved through the room, noting faces, positions, the work left unfinished.

"We need a word," she said. "In private."

Sakura sent Dustin and Sybil out for the market run early, and they left without question.

Sakura and Thall stepped forward together.

Liang let the doors rest closed before turning back to them. His attention went first to Sakura.

"You have done Hanzhong proud," he said.

Sakura inclined into a respectful bow. "I was guided well."

Liang turned then, his focus narrowing onto Thall. "Now," he said, "we will speak carefully. Walls listen, even when they appear kind."

He stepped closer, near enough that distance no longer softened intent. His eyes stayed on Thall. Aika followed.

"According to the Dominion," Liang said quietly, "you are already dead."

◆ ◆ ◆

Thall frowned. "Dead?"

"Yes." Liang answered.

Liang did not rush the explanation. "A month ago, a Dominion dispatch reached the temple. They asked about a messenger sent from Serenthall some time back." His gaze did not waver. "Their report placed him crossing into Hanzhong. Witnesses noted him the following morning near the market stalls, collapsing and taken into temple care."

Aika's expression remained unchanged, but her attention sharpened.

"Later," Liang continued, "someone matching his description was seen at a tavern on the western lane."

He paused.

"That tavern burned not long after. Several died. One body could not be identified. No name was claimed."

Silence pressed in around them, dense enough to feel.

"The messenger's name was Thall," Liang said. "According to record, his family has not heard from him since."

Thall stood still, attention drawn inward, the room passing around him without reach.

Sakura drew a breath. "But he—"

"Why?" Aika asked, cutting in without raising her voice. "Why did you remain silent for five years?"

Thall met her gaze. He did not look away.

"At first, I wasn't ready," he said. "After that, I kept pushing the thought of home farther off and stayed busy. It was easier to keep moving."

Aika studied him for a long moment. "So you were not hiding here," she said. "And it was not intent that kept you from them."

"No," Thall said. "It wasn't."

After a brief pause, Aika spoke again. "The Kingdom of Aetherwind does not intend to correct the Dominion." Her eyes stayed on him. "We will not challenge their record."

Liang inclined his head slightly. "Nor will the Lianhua Dynasty."

Aika continued without pause. "But we will not hide you knowingly."

She turned her head slightly, just enough to include Liang without breaking focus.

"Aetherwind's standing with the Dominion is already strained," Aika said. "Trade lanes are watched. Messengers questioned. Any sign that we shelter someone the Dominion has marked would carry consequence beyond the Hollow."

Her gaze returned to Thall. "You will need to leave."

The words were plain. Final.

Sakura took half a step forward. "He can't just be sent out. Not now. Not after—"

Liang lifted one hand. Not in rebuke, but in boundary.

"Sakura," he said quietly.

She stopped.

"As a resident under Lianhua protection," Liang continued, "you are not permitted to accompany him. Not beyond this place. Not under these circumstances."

Her breath caught, sharp and audible.

Aika did not soften. "This is not punishment," she said. "It is reality. If you remain here, the Hollow remains will not remain untouched."

Silence followed, heavy and exact.

Thall inclined his head once. "How long do I have?"

"Until nightfall tomorrow," Aika said. "You will leave without escort and without notice."

Sakura looked to Liang. He did not meet her eyes.

When Thall turned toward her, she was already watching him.

Chapter 28: Up In Flames

Aika turned to leave.

"High Priest," Thall said.

The word cut clean through the practice. All attention returned to him at once. Aika stopped. Liang paused beside her. Sakura looked up, breath caught.

Thall did not rush his next words. "I have one request."

Aika faced him fully. "Speak."

"I was denied my rite of passage," he said. "At five years old. I lived under the Dominion." His voice remained even. "Before I leave, I ask to complete it here. Properly."

Liang's eyes narrowed slightly, not in refusal, but in calculation. He looked to Aika. She met his gaze. For a moment, nothing passed between them that could be seen.

Then Aika nodded once.

"We will allow it," she said. "At day's end. Tonight."

Relief did not touch Thall's face. He inclined his head in acknowledgment.

"Bring only those you trust," Aika continued. "Few. This is not a spectacle."

"I understand."

Aika turned and left. Liang followed without another word.

Silence returned, thinner now.

Sakura spoke first. "You're not going alone."

Thall looked at her. "Sakura—"

She stepped closer. "The ring binds us," she said quietly. "You do not walk away from me, and I do not remain behind."

He searched her face, then shook his head once. "I need to find ground first. Somewhere stable. I won't ask you to follow into uncertainty."

She did not move. Her voice wavered, held together by effort, eyes bright as she fought for control. "Then I will wait until you call. But I will not stay apart."

For a long moment, he said nothing. Then he nodded. "I'll send word as soon as I can."

Her composure broke. She leaned into him, forehead pressed to his chest, tears coming without sound. He wrapped an arm around her and brushed his fingers through her hair, slow and steady, until her breathing eased.

A voice sounded from the corridor. A patient, hesitant.

Sakura straightened at once. She wiped her face with the back of her hand, drew a breath, and turned toward the hall. "I'm coming," she said, already moving.

Thall watched her go then slipped away without drawing notice.

In his room, he prepared in silence.

Half an hour later, Sybil and Dustin returned from the market, arms full. They set their bundles down and spoke in low tones, trading notes and accounts.

The hollow did not wait before; it will not wait now.

◆ ◆ ◆

That evening, near the outer ring, a summoner stood at the edge of the training yard with Lea. Ashe waited at her side, calm and watchful.

"That's too soon," Lea said. "I don't think you're ready."

The summoner kept his eyes on the yard. "I'm comfortable with it," he replied. "Readiness isn't comfort."

Lea opened her mouth to answer, then stopped as footsteps approached.

Olivia slowed as she reached them, bow in hand. "Can I ask you something?" she said, glancing between them. "About my aim."

The summoner stepped back at once. "I'll think on it," he said to Lea. Then he nodded and left the yard.

Lea exhaled and motioned Olivia forward. They crossed to the archery line, where targets stood scarred and sun-bleached. Ethan lingered nearby, already nocking an arrow of his own.

Olivia set her stance and drew, posture tight with effort.

Lea stepped in beside her, adjusted her footing with a light touch, then tilted her elbow just enough to ease the strain. "Let the ground carry you," Lea said. "Don't fight it."

When Olivia loosed, the arrow struck wide but clean.

Ethan released almost at the same time, his shot flying fast and erratic.

Lea turned her head. "Slow down," she said. "One true arrow is worth more than a handful sent in haste."

They trained, arrows thudding into wood, small corrections offered without fuss. The sun climbed higher before anyone noticed.

Dustin appeared at the edge of the yard, breath a little quick. "Lea," he called. "Thall is asking for the three of you."

Lea nodded once and lowered her bow.

Lea reached the practice with Dustin, Olivia, and Ethan close behind her. Sakura stood near the central table with Thall.

Thall inclined his head in thanks as they entered.

Not long after, Sybil came in, saying she could not find Master Roland.

Thall paused, eyes moving over the room. "This will do."

Sakura crossed the floor and secured the main door, the latch sounding final in the quiet.

Thall cleared his throat. "I'm sorry to call you all at this hour," he said. "I wouldn't have, if it weren't necessary." His gaze moved around the room. "What I'm about to say isn't small. I asked you here because you're the ones I trust most."

Lea spoke first. "This has to do with the Dominion." It wasn't a question. She glanced at the others. "You didn't call anyone who would argue otherwise."

Thall did not deny it. "It does." He drew a breath. "According to the Dominion, I'm dead. I was informed earlier today." The words landed and stayed. "On paper, I no longer exist. Aetherwind has offered me citizenship under a new name."

The room went quiet at once.

From the corner, Lea spoke. "Are you certain?"

He nodded.

"I was there for all of it," Sakura said quietly.

Sybil's eyes widened. "That's why you were visited," she said. "By the High Priest."

Thall cleared his throat again. "There's more. I'll be completing the Rite tonight."

"I can put things aside," Lea said without pause.

One by one, the others agreed, voices low but sure.

Thall bowed his head, breath leaving him in a quiet release. He did not tell them about what followed.

◆ ◆ ◆

Not long after, they gathered inside the temple of Guardian's Hollow.

Candles lit the space, their glow kept low and deliberate. Only those who had been told were allowed inside. High

Priest Aika assigned a young priest she trusted to stand watch at the entrance, admitting each person with a glance and a nod, turning away anyone who did not belong. High Priest Liang waited, silent and attentive.

When all were present, Aika turned to Thall.

"Before we begin," she said, "you must choose who you honor."

He did not pause.

"The Sun God," he said. "Solithar."

The tension in the room eased, not into comfort, but into alignment.

Aika inclined her head once. Liang followed.

Sand had been laid in a wide circle across the temple floor, pale and fine. Each grain had been blessed by Aika's hand before it touched the stone. It did not lie flat. It responded to presence rather than pressure.

Aika stepped to its edge and placed her right hand over her heart, her left open toward the circle.

"Solithar," she said, voice steady, "who rises without summons and sets without leave. Witness what stands before you."

Thall stepped forward.

He crossed the boundary and came to rest at the center. At Aika's slight gesture, he turned and presented his back, shoulders bare, spine straight, breath even.

"Let what has endured be known," Aika said. "Let what was denied be answered. Let no doctrine bar what was never granted by it."

The sand glowed faintly, then dimmed.

Nothing stirred.

Aika turned toward Liang, composure slipping for the first time, her eyes searching his face.

Then the sand lifted.

It hovered mid-air.

Across the room, no one moved. Breath paused. Eyes fixed as a red glow traced its slow, deliberate path.

True flame came to life, contained and disciplined, unmistakably alive. It traced the lines with purpose, marking flesh without heat or pain. Each stroke claimed through intent rather than display.

Neither Aika nor Liang spoke.

When the mark finished, it did not fade.

It remained, etched into Thall's back as though it had always waited there, a living imprint bound to skin and blood alike. The flame drew inward, taken into him without resistance.

Aika lowered her hand.

"Solithar," she said, voice steady, "you who watch without demand and burn without malice. What was taken has been returned. What was denied has been named. Let this mark stand as witness, not of dominion, but of will freely chosen."

The mark stood clear upon Thall's back.

Solithar had answered.

Chapter 29: The Shape of Absence

High Priest Aika stepped back, her hands drawing in close at her sides.

The symbol did not fade from his back.

He turned toward Aika. "Thank you," he said. "What symbol have I received?"

No one answered.

Aika's breath caught, just enough to be seen. Liang did not move, his gaze fixed on Thall's back. Around the room, shoulders tightened, eyes averted and then drawn back again, as if looking too long might invite consequence.

Dustin leaned toward Olivia and whispered, far too loud for the space, "Is this an Eldhar thing?"

Olivia did not look at him. "The mark is," she murmured. "It staying is not."

Something in the room drew taut.

At last, Liang spoke. "Thall," he said. "That is how you will be recorded."

He paused.

"But you will be known by your blessing," Liang continued. "By the mark granted to you."

Thall lifted his gaze, searching faces before words.

Aika stepped forward. "The mark remains," she said. "There will be no record made. No form can contain this."

A moment later, Sakura spoke. "Thall."

She moved closer, close enough that he did not need to turn. Her voice stayed even. "You have been granted the Fire-Heart."

He drew a slow breath and let it out through his nose.

"The Fire-Heart," he repeated. Not a question. He shook his head once.

"It is true," Lea said.

She stepped in beside him. "It doesn't change who you are," she said. "It doesn't erase what came before. It confirms it."

Sakura drew in a breath and released it without speaking.

Aika raised her hand. "The Rite is concluded."

For a moment longer, no one moved.

The younger tamers hesitated, glancing toward the High Priests before lowering their eyes again.

Sakura brought him his shirt.

He pulled it on, movements controlled, his back kept straight as if the mark carried weight of its own. When he turned toward the exit, the space opened without a word.

Sakura and Lea walked with him from the temple, their pace aligned. Behind them, the room did not follow. Some watched him go. Others turned away only after he passed the threshold.

◆ ◆ ◆

By the time they reached the practice, the lamps were already lit and the air had cooled.

They took their places around the kitchen table. Ashe taking a corner downstairs.

The room quieted until Thall spoke. "It isn't what we're given," he said, more to himself than to them. "It's what we do with it."

Lea and Sakura turned toward him.

"I don't have to hide," he continued. "I won't run from this."

His words lingered.

He drew a deeper breath, then looked to Lea. "There is one more thing. Something the High Priests told Sakura and me earlier today." He paused, letting the weight of it settle. "I am to leave the Hollow. If I am found alive, my presence will draw attention the Dominion will not ignore."

Lea did not answer at once. She leaned back slightly, eyes on the table, then looked to Sakura and back to Thall.

"That's why you chose to complete the Rite," she nodded, then asked "when do you go?"

He shook his head. "I have until nightfall tomorrow."

Lea studied him a moment longer, then nodded once. "Then leaving is the right choice."

Sakura's breath caught. "Lea—"

Lea lifted her hand, not to stop her, but to ask for patience. "Listen first."

Her gaze returned to Thall. "The Hollow is not as secure as it appears. It hasn't been for some time." She drew a breath. "I didn't know how to say it before. Or who to say it to."

Thall waited.

"Since I began working closely with Roland," she continued, "I noticed patterns. Messages arriving without record. Routes that didn't match supply or patrol needs. He grew guarded where he once was open." Her mouth tightened. "That is why I've been distracted."

Sakura stared at her. "You never said—"

"I wasn't certain," Lea said. "Not yet."

She looked down, then back up. "The day I was late. The day you spoke to Sakura about your feelings." Her voice did not waver. "I followed Roland."

The room went still.

"I kept distance. I listened," Lea said, eyes on Thall. "He met with a messenger outside the walls. Not a trader. Not a courier from Aetherwind."

Thall did not interrupt.

"He carried Dominion markings," Lea said. "Hidden with care. But I know what I saw."

Sakura shook her head once, disbelief plain. "Roland wouldn't—"

"If the Master Tamer is receiving Dominion messages," Lea said quietly, "then the Hollow is already compromised. Whatever protection we believe we have is thinner than we think."

Silence followed, heavier than before.

Thall's gaze drifted, unfocused for a moment. When he spoke again, his voice was low. "I was afraid of this." He looked back to them. "I've noticed the changes too. The tightened control. The way information no longer moves cleanly."

Sakura said nothing.

Thall pushed his chair back and stood. The movement was calm, deliberate. "Then I know what I need to do."

Both of them looked up.

"I leave," he said. "Not as retreat, but as distance." His eyes were clear now. "If the Dominion is watching this place, then my absence becomes silence. And silence gives us room to see what they believe they already own."

Sakura rose slowly.

Thall turned to her. "I won't disappear," he said. "I will move carefully. I will send word. And when I return, it will be because we are ready."

Lea nodded once.

Sakura looked at him, worry plain now, not fear but the weight of what lay ahead. He met her gaze and stayed there, steady enough for both of them.

Lea spoke again. "We need to control what spreads."

They turned toward her.

"I'll speak with my trainees," she said. "Olivia and Ethan. They'll keep the Rite to themselves. No speculation. No retelling."

"I'll do the same with Sybil and Dustin," Sakura said.

Lea nodded. "No one else. Not Roland. Not Harlan. Not anyone who thinks they're helping by asking questions."

Sakura's jaw tightened, but she agreed.

"I'll remain here," Sakura said after a moment. "At least for now." She looked to Thall. "Once you find a place, I'll make arrangements. Anything that needs to be cleared or moved, I'll handle it." She hesitated. "Through Corvin Holt. He should know ahead of time."

Thall considered it. "Holt," he said. "Can we trust him?"

Lea answered without pause. "Yes."

They both looked at her.

"I had the same concern," Lea said. "A trader is always a risk. I checked him in the past. Routes. Partners. Patterns. He is what he appears to be, practical, self-interested, and reliable." Her mouth curved faintly. "Those are the safest kinds."

Sakura let out a breath she had been holding.

Thall nodded. "Then we tell Holt."

He looked back to Lea. "And you."

"I'll stay until Sakura leaves," Lea said. "After that, I'll handle whatever follows."

There was no bravado in the answer. Only resolve.

Sakura reached for Thall's hand. Her fingers closed around his. He turned slightly toward her, grounding himself in the contact.

None of them spoke for a while. The decisions stood on their own.

Night drew in around the Hollow.

Lea rose first. "We should rest." She paused at the doorway and looked back at them. "Good night."

"Good night," Sakura said.

"Good night," Thall replied.

Lea left, her steps fading down the corridor.

A moment passed.

Then Thall pushed his chair back and stood. Sakura followed a heartbeat later. She did not speak at once. She held his gaze, something unsteady moving behind her eyes.

"May I stay with you tonight," she asked quietly. "In your room."

He smiled, soft and unmistakable. "I would like that."

Relief crossed her face before she hid it.

They walked the hall together without hurry. When they reached his door, neither hesitated. The room was dark and spare, the window open just enough to carry the night air.

Chapter 30: What Answers Back

Thall woke before dawn.

For a moment, he did not move. Sakura lay beside him, still asleep, her hand wrapped around his. He kept his breathing slow, unwilling to pull her from rest.

In sleep, she looked different. Not guarded, nor precise. There was a faint crease between her brows, as if even here something troubled her. He watched light creep along the wall as the sky brightened, brushing the edge of her face, catching in her dark hair where it lay between them.

The light reached her eyes at last. She stirred, lashes lifting as she saw him watching and smiled.

Then memory reached her. The smile faltered.

She sat up too quickly, then froze as she remembered undressing the night before. She made a small sound and dropped back beneath the covers at once, pulling them close.

Thall laughed under his breath. He turned away, drawing the blanket with him as he rose. "I'll give you the room," he said, already moving toward the washroom.

She waited long enough to be sure he was gone, then gathered her robes and slipped into the other washroom down the hall.

Thall finished first. He dressed, strapped his sword, and began sorting what he would take with him. He kept the rest neat, as if order might make leaving easier.

A knock sounded at the open doorframe.

Lea leaned there, arms folded. "Sounded like someone didn't sleep alone," she said lightly.

Heat rose in his face at once.

She smiled and stepped inside. "Relax. I'm glad for you."

They packed together quietly, passing items back and forth without comment.

Sakura joined them a short while later and helped until voices rose from below. "Sybil and Dustin are already downstairs," she said. "I'll make breakfast."

Thall nodded. Lea did not look up.

They worked until the kettle began to sing.

They sat together at the table, eggs steaming, bread warm, tea poured. No one spoke at first.

"This might be the last time for a while," Sakura said at last. Her voice stayed even, but her eyes shone.

Lea opened her mouth, then closed it again.

Thall reached for Sakura's hand. "I'll find a place," he said. "Soon. When I do, we'll be together again."

She nodded and pressed her lips together.

After they finished eating, Lea gathered the dishes; Thall returned to his room to finish sorting what remained, and Sakura went downstairs to speak with Sybil and Dustin about the day ahead.

◆ ◆ ◆

A soft tap sounded at the kitchen window. Then another.

Lea looked up, recognizing a bird perched on the sill.

She crossed the room and opened the window, but the bird lifted at once and flew. Lea watched it cross the yard and land on the shoulder of a figure half-lost in shadow. A bow rested in their hand.

They pulled on the string, then an arrow struck the outer wall of the window, clean and deliberate. A folded letter was bound to the shaft.

By the time Lea looked back down, the figure was gone.

She reached for the arrow, easing the shaft free and working the binding loose with steady fingers. The letter came away cleanly.

She unrolled it.

There was a single line of writing, neat and deliberate.

Summoners summoned, Tamers tamed; Invokers woke the elemental grain.

Below it lay a rough map, ink pressed with purpose rather than care. One marker stood out, circled twice. Lea traced it with her finger.

Southeast of Faunacre. Southwest of Zhìyé village.

Farther south than either road would normally take a traveler. Beyond patrol routes. Beyond formal claim. Outside any border she knew.

Her pulse quickened.

This was what she had been waiting for, though she had never named it aloud. Proof that the line drawn between call and command was not as fixed as they claimed. That something existed beyond division.

She folded the map and letter together heading towards Thall's door, it stood open.

He looked up as she entered.

"I think you may have a destination," she said.

He straightened. "From who?"

She held up the folded paper. "Someone who has been watching me for a long time."

He did not interrupt.

She told him about the bird. How it first appeared when she was still in the orphanage. How it returned over the years without pattern, never startled, never driven away. Always watching. Always waiting. She told him how she came to believe it was not bound to tamers or summoners, not in the way the world insisted.

"I think there is something else," she said. "Something older, or maybe simply ignored."

Thall listened without comment. When she finished, he asked one question. "Do you trust the one who sent this?"

Lea looked down at the folded map. "I want to," she said. "But I don't know if I should. It could be a lure... Or worse."

Silence stretched between them.

At last, Thall nodded. "Then we go prepared."

She looked up.

"I don't have anything tying me here now," he continued. "If someone has been waiting for the right moment, they may have known that." He glanced toward the window, the yard beyond. "But we don't walk into it blind."

Lea let out a breath she had not realized she was holding. "Carefully," she said.

He nodded in agreement.

◆ ◆ ◆

They stood for a moment, the decision resting between them.

"Nightfall," Lea said.

"Yes," Thall replied. "Under cover of dark."

Lea hesitated. "And Sakura."

Thall shook his head once. "Not yet. We keep this between us for now. We'll tell her when we know what it is."

Lea weighed it, then nodded. "All right."

Thall returned to his pack, sorting again, this time reducing it to what mattered. He worked with care, not haste.

"Get what we'll need from the market," he said. "Before it closes."

Lea agreed and left the room.

Downstairs, Sakura stood near the practice space, watching Sybil and Dustin tend to a patient. Lea paused only long enough to find Ashe and draw him close, then slipped out.

Sakura could not focus.

Her attention drifted no matter how she tried to draw it back. She followed the treatment by habit, hands moving where needed, words spoken when required, but her thoughts remained elsewhere.

Dustin waited until the patient had gone. Then he turned to her. "You should take the day," he said. "We can handle things."

Sybil glanced up and nodded.

Sakura did not argue. She thanked them and stepped away.

She headed for the messenger tower instead.

The clerk barely looked up as Sakura prepared the bird. She kept the note brief.

I would like to speak with you regarding supplies. If you are able, please stop by.

She sealed it and sent the bird on its way.

On her return, raised voices carried down the street.

A summoner stood at the center of it, a wind elemental coiled at his side, its edges visible in the dust it stirred. He shouted about exaggeration and fear, about how the Dominion was not the monster people claimed. Opposite him, a tamer stood with a fox at heel, answering each claim with anger barely contained.

The crowd thickened.

The wind snapped without warning.

The elemental struck, a sharp force that caught the fox full in the side and hurled it across the stones. Blood spattered the ground.

Chaos followed.

The tamer ran, dropping to his knees beside the fox, hands shaking as he tried to gather it close. The summoner turned away and walked off as if nothing had happened.

Sakura was already moving.

She knelt beside the fox, the smell of blood sharp and sudden. The crowd pressed in, voices rising.

She hesitated.

Then she drew a breath and spoke an incantation, careful and precise, hands steady as she pressed against the wound. She looked up at the tamer. "Come with me," she said. "Now."

He nodded, tears streaking his face, barely holding himself together as he followed her toward the practice.

Sybil reached them first, already working as Sakura guided the fox down. Dustin arrived moments later with herbs in his arms.

The tamer paced a few steps away, sobbing openly.

Sakura stayed firm, voice steady as she continued the incantation. Sybil worked the ointments into the wounds. Dustin passed what was needed without a word.

But the injuries ran too deep.

The fox shuddered once, then lay still.

Sakura felt the life leave it beneath her hands.

For a moment, no one spoke.

The tamer collapsed forward, a sound breaking from him that had no shape to it. Sakura remained where she was, hands unmoving, eyes fixed on the fox she could not save.

Outside, the noise of the street pressed on, unchanged.

Dedication

For my wife,

who stood beside me through thick and thin.

Through sickness, uncertainty, and the long stretches when patience was tested.

You never complained. You never asked for anything in return.

You supported me with a smile, even when the weight was heavy and the days were not kind.

You were a blessing to me as a wife.

Steady when I faltered, patient when I struggled, and present in ways that mattered more than words.

You carried more than your share without ever making it feel like a burden.

And beyond that, you have been a blessing as a mother to our children.

Your love for them is constant and generous.

You protect them, guide them, and give them joy, even when you are tired, even when no one is watching.

They are who they are because of you.

This book exists because you stood with me.

Our family stands because you do.

Thank you for staying, for believing, and for loving all of us so completely.